PRINCE OF SPRING

By Mahir Salih

Contents

Chapter 1: Blood on the Promenade
Chapter 2: The Aftermath
Chapter 3: The Escape
Chapter 4: Heat of the Desert
Chapter 5: Lac Léman
Chapter 6: Conspiring at The Ritz
Chapter 7: The Fugitive
Chapter 8: The Chaos
Chapter 9: Buenos Aires
Chapter 10: In the Dragon's Den
Chapter 11: The Sand Castle
Chapter 12: The Silk Route
Chapter 13: Bad News
Chapter 14: Stars in the Desert
Chapter 15: Hit and Run
Chapter 16: Poison in the Well
Chapter 17: A Friend in Need
Chapter 18: Company Business
Chapter 19: The Gates of Hell
Chapter 20: A Helping Hand
Chapter 21: Nowhere to Hide
Chapter 22: A Deal with the Devil
Chapter 23: Enemy at the Gates
Chapter 24: No Heroes

Chapter 1
Blood on the Promenade

At 4am local time, a private jet arrived on the French Riviera, touching down at Nice Côte D'Azur Airport. Later that day, the thermometer would climb to the high 30s Celsius, as was typical of summer in the South of France. At this early hour, however, the sky was pitch black, the air fresh and cool.

International dignitaries were a common sight on the tarmac at Nice, business as usual for the French police and security forces. But tonight the security presence was stronger than ever, with the airport on red alert – indicating an imminent terrorist attack. The civilian staff, meanwhile, were somewhat indifferent to all the hustle and bustle. After all, since the 9/11 attacks, they'd seen more than enough alerts. Before the day was out, many of them would reassess their attitude.

As soon as the jet touched down, a team of French security personnel appeared by the plane's steps. The door opened, and a huge man appeared, sporting a thick beard to match his bulging muscles. He pushed his way through the pretty hostesses, whose makeup was still perfect, despite the early hour. The bearded man was followed by several others who seemed to be identical twins in terms of muscle mass.

After a wait of some minutes, a slim, handsome, middle-aged man appeared amongst them. He was six-feet tall, dark-haired and with a small, well-manicured goatee beard. His hazel eyes were hidden behind a pair of Ray Ban sunglasses. He walked down the steps with a slow, unsteady gait, resembling the tentative first steps of a toddler. His face and figure were not unknown to the Western media. In previous years, photographs of the man had appeared on the front pages of tabloid newspapers – mainly the British ones. There had been no shortage of news about his whereabouts, love life, adventures and extravagant lifestyle to entertain the readers.

Prince Ali really did seem to be struggling this morning, walking like an old man, hardly exhibiting the lively, ballet-dancing steps of the past. Gone was the peacock-like strut of the young man groomed to inherit his father's throne. This morning, of course, he had numerous excuses, including a hectic 24 hours of phone calls and business meetings in London – but alcohol was playing a big part. Since the so-called Arab Spring, which had brought turbulence to his country and the Middle East, alcohol had been Ali's best friend.

Following close behind the prince as he descended the steps was an equally handsome young man, also sporting Ray Bans. This was Ali's son, Shehab, a mere 21 years old and the apple of his father's eye. The youth, though hardly brash, had not yet lost the spring in his step.

Waiting on the tarmac was a Rolls Royce for the visitors, along with a small reception party, including the deputy mayor. On his previous visits, both official and private, Ali might have been greeted by the mayor, perhaps even a minister – but those days were long gone.

The car hit the road, heading for downtown Nice. He would check into the Negresco, where the hotel manager's welcome was always warm, and perhaps at last he could get some sleep. There was just one more meeting on the schedule – dinner with a local businessman – and then the holiday would begin. A short hop to Saint-Tropez and finally some rest.

As they sped along the Promenade des Anglais with its view of the Mediterranean Sea, the prince was flooded with an array of conflicting emotions. There was calmness, but also anger. Strongest of all, as the sea air blew through the air conditioning and into his nostrils, there was nostalgia for his homeland. He was transported back to that small emirate in the days of British rule, before the oil boom. A movie began to play in his mind: his first swimming lessons; riding his horse; his first sexual encounter – with a private servant...

Ali's thoughts were interrupted by the crack of gunfire, followed by a huge impact that forced the Rolls Royce off the road. There was more gunfire and frantic shouting in French and Arabic, and the wailing of police sirens. He tried to move but found himself wedged tight against something, a searing pain in his chest. The pure scent of the sea breeze had been replaced by the smell of smoke. He felt a warm liquid on his face.

Semi-conscious now, he continued to reminisce about his early childhood. His deceased mother called to him, touching his warm forehead. He had missed her badly. She had departed for the other side while giving birth to his sister. She had already suffered eclampsia while giving birth to Ali, and the British gynaecologist had warned her against another pregnancy. She departed the world trying to provide Ali with a brother to support him when he ascended to the throne. Alas, Ali had had to survive alone in a sea of sharks.

He began talking to his mother, her presence accompanied by the scent of her favourite perfume, Dehn Al-Oudh.

'Mummy,' he said, 'I want to be with you.'

He heard her soft, kind voice penetrating his ear drums.

'Not yet, son. Not yet.'

She vanished over the horizon and Ali was alone again.

Chapter 2
The Aftermath

Ali opened his eyes to find himself lying beneath a white sheet stained with drops of blood. The smell of the Mediterranean breeze penetrated to his sinuses. He thought for a moment that he was still in his car on the Promenade des Anglais. Then the sound of traffic outside the window brought him to his senses – like a pinch ending a dream.

He had no idea of the time, whether day or night. Not that this was an entirely new sensation; since losing his throne, he had become somewhat accustomed to feeling adrift.

Suddenly, a slim figure dashed into the room – like a butterfly flitting from one flower to another. It was a young, blonde nurse, resembling an angel in her white gown. She greeted him with an adorable smile, like Juliette Binoche, but softer.

'Bonjour,' she said.

He shook his head in disbelief. He had been surrounded by tough Arab security men with thick moustaches, and now he was in heaven with the angels.

He replied in Arabic, offering the typical morning greeting: 'Sabah al-khayr.'

The sunshine was pouring through the window, causing his pupils to shrink to small dots. The kind nurse headed for the curtains, aiming to close them. Ali stopped her, waving his hands as he contemplated the deep, blue sea. For a moment, it seemed he was in his palace overlooking the ocean. But that wasn't possible.

He asked himself what a French nurse was doing here. He normally relied on English, American or Arab nurses, not French ones. The sudden appearance of the French language was disorienting.

He recalled his early years as a student of French at the Institut Le Rosey in Rolle, Switzerland. As one of the elite students – mainly royalty – from the Middle East, Africa and the Far East, he had been proud of his mastery of the language. Yes, he knew French well.

'Bonjour Mademoiselle,' Ali said in his polished Swiss accent. 'Where am I?'

'You're in Lenval Hospital in Nice, Your Highness,' explained the nurse. She pointed through the window to the view.

His country's close links to Britain meant the adoption of the protocols of the British monarchy, and yet he wasn't sure that he still qualified as a 'Royal Highness'. He had not sat on a throne for a year now, and would likely never do so again.

He tried to turn in the direction of the nurse, but his bruised body was hurting, and he cried out in pain. He had clearly been injured, but exactly where and how was a mystery.

Confusion turned to fear, and he began to yell: 'Why am I here? What happened? Why am I in hospital?'

The poor nurse wasn't prepared for an interrogation from a prince. 'I believe you've had an accident,' she said.

He picked up the word 'accident' – but before he could question her further, she left the room in haste.

Patience is a virtue, but not for Ali. Like a child, he started to kick-off. He wanted to speak with his embassy or with whoever might be in charge. Where was his entourage? He pressed the red button next to his bed, triggering an alarm that shattered the tranquility of the hospital.

A middle-aged Frenchman in a white coat entered, followed by two security guards and two male nurses. They tried to restrain the agitated prince, but it was difficult. He roared like an injured tiger. After some wrestling, Ali succumbed to the kind, reassuring words of the doctor, tender words in English but with a heavy French accent.

'Please calm down,' he said.

Ali responded with a big jerking movement of his body. 'Tell me what happened!' he demanded.

'You had an accident,' said the doctor.

'When and where?'

'It happened last night.'

Ali was muddled by the doctor's accent – and the concussion wasn't helping.

'What do you mean by an accident?' Ali whispered in disbelief.

A tall, fair-haired Frenchman, suited and booted in the elegant old-fashioned style, stepped forward, brushing the poor doctor aside. Ali assumed the man to be a detective, or perhaps an intelligence official. Either way, he found the man's boldness somewhat shocking. After all, Ali was used to being the only prima donna in the room. Nevertheless, he was keen to learn about the mysterious events that had landed him in a hospital bed.

'Monsieur, there was an attempt on your life,' said the man.

Ali was angered more by the directness of the statement than the dreadful situation in which he found himself.

'Out with it!' he shouted. 'Who wants to harm me?'

'We are not sure. The French intelligence is working on …'

Ali interrupted him impatiently: 'What happened to my entourage, my bodyguards and chauffeurs?'

The prince could not recall his last contact with bodyguards and chauffeurs; the recent past was a blank. However, he knew such people were never far from his side.

'Unfortunately, they are either dead or injured,' the well-dressed man replied.

Ali shouted back, employing the posh, public-school accent he had mastered at Eton and Oxford: 'What do you mean? I am Prince Ali! How dare you and your government treat me like this!'

The well-dressed French official was clearly taken by surprise. His Gallic temper was just on the point of surfacing when the doctor ordered everyone to leave the room. He gave a sign to the nurse, who injected Ali with a tranquilizer, assisted by two hospital porters.

While Ali was very much in the dark about recent events, the same could not be said of the general population of France. The media had gone into a frenzy, with TV5 providing rolling coverage of the extraordinary occurrence in Nice. The French still harboured a guilt complex over the death of Princess Diana in 1997, and they were keen not to have another prominent royal killed on their soil.

The story of the attempt on Ali's life was indeed shocking. Here was a man forced to give up his throne in order to avoid bloodshed – forced to relinquish control of this tiny, oil-funded principality due a military coup orchestrated by his own family. And now, while pursuing a new life in exile, an assault was made on his life – and that of his teenage son.

The news reports were peppered with potted histories of Jawhar, a place most French citizens would struggle to find on a map. The nation's modern history had begun with Ali's great-grandfather, who was appointed head of the fledgling state with the blessing of the British. They had declared that small corner of the world a British protectorate. And in return for their protection, the British had been granted the rights to exploit the oil beneath the golden desert sands. The significance of the country's name, meaning 'jewel' in Arabic, was not lost on the colonial masters.

Three generations later, long after independence, Ali lost his throne in the flames of the Arab Spring, that wave of uprisings launched in early 2011. A rather distant brother – by a different mother – took over, providing a quick fix, a facelift to the ailing mediaeval regime. However, the brother didn't last long and was himself replaced by a distant cousin, the weak and inexperienced Prince Yousef.

Ali had gone into exile, first in Dubai, then moving in wider circles, flitting between London, Paris and New York – occasionally heading for the seaside. Accompanying him into exile was Shehab, his eldest son, the boy who had once represented the family's hopes for the future. For the past year, they had been constant companions on the road.

Before the Arab Spring, Ali had been preparing Shehab to take over the throne. However, events had taken a wrong turn, and those hopes were dashed. The father had suffered the humiliation of a coup d'état; the son was denied his birthright.

Ali had cherished his son, openly showing his affection for the boy, quite in contravention of the Arab tradition, particularly in royal households.

Ali's own upbringing had been somewhat different, the father-son relationship typically distant. The father, of course, wanted Ali to grow up strong, prepared for his future role as leader. The princess consort, meanwhile, was mostly concerned with protecting her son from conspiracies, including the wide range of accidents that were just waiting to happen. She worked hard at protecting Ali, who was, after all, her only hope of obtaining power or recognition in a male-dominated society. It had been the same for Ali's grandmother and his great-grandmother, who ruled the family, tribe and country in the past.

On ascending to the throne, Ali had repeated the traditional pattern, producing a male heir to take his place. The boy was the product of a loveless marriage, an arranged union with a cousin aimed at resolving a political conflict within the family. Despite the loveless nature of this marriage, Ali had loved his son deeply – longing for his security and success. Indeed, Shehab's safety had been Ali's prime concern.

Through the drug-induced torpor, Ali opened his eyes and stared at the ceiling, a wave of panic spreading through mind and body. Where was his son? The boy had been in the car with him. It was all coming back now; they had been on their way from the airport, sitting side by side in the back of the Rolls Royce. Then the gunfire and smoke and blood – the boy's blood on his face.

Ali tried to speak, but his words were garbled; he tried to swing out of bed, but he managed only a clumsy roll to one side, bashing against the guard rail. Summoning all his energy, he began to shout, pouring forth a mix of Arabic, English and French.

Asserting his authority, the doctor ushered everyone from the room, ignoring the protests of the arrogant detective, who seemed to enjoy humiliating people.

'Come on, leave quickly,' said the doctor. 'The nurse will give him another injection.'

The doctor pressed the buzzer and two broad-shouldered porters in white coats entered. They each took hold of an arm and held Ali firmly. The nurse prepared a dose of Lorazepam and plunged the needle into the patient's arm.

All the royal etiquette was out of the window now, as the prince poured forth a string of violent threats. 'I will execute you all!' he shouted, perfectly in tune with his former role as head of state.

Soon, however, the threats were replaced with sorrowful pleas to see his son. 'Where is he? I want to see my boy! Please! Where's my boy?'

Eventually, the medication took hold. The prince knew when he was beaten; his limbs went limp and he settled deep into the mattress. The tears rolled down his face, like the tears of a war-widow on learning of her loss. Tears of this sort were, of course, in conflict with the macho, stiff-upper-lip tradition of Arab males, not to mention royalty – but he simply could not help it.

The room became narrower and darker, and in no time he was lost in his dreams. He was watching a movie trailer of his former life, including scenes from his various marriages – four wives in all. He saw his sweet, obedient mother too. She was caressing him, just as she used to, stealing a minute to express her affection, against the orders of her husband, who was busy foiling plots or over-indulging with his mistresses and younger wives.

Suddenly, Ali was a grown man, defending his throne from assault. The Arab Spring had started, spreading through North Africa and the Arab world, spreading like a fire from house to house. The prince was under immense pressure – both from his family and the newly formed Peoples' Council.

Ali resisted up to the last minute, under fire from his usual allies, including the normally supportive Western governments. He resisted in vain, forced finally to concede defeat and flee, burdened by an overwhelming sense of failure, of humiliation. In Arab culture, a man without dignity does not deserve to live – and Ali had lost his dignity and everything besides.

And now it was all over; he was a fugitive in southern France. In his dream, he was running along the Promenade des Anglais, ducking down the backstreets, searching for a place to hide, looking for his son, who might be dead but was surely lurking nearby.

To the nurse, as she stood watching, the patient was sleeping peacefully, finally at rest. The doctor had already departed and was busily updating the assembled officials on Ali's progress. The nurse pulled the curtains, blocking out the sunshine and the deep, blue sea, then padded softly from the room.

Chapter 3
The Escape

It was a hot August day in Saint-Tropez, pearl of the Côte D'Azur, that most glamorous corner of the world to which the rich and famous flocked each year. As one Arab explorer once observed, the inhabitants of this part of the world would not go to Paradise – because they already lived in one.

The French town took its name from a saint executed by the Romans for adopting Christianity. Through its long history, the place had been home to Greeks, Romans, Arabs and Italians, drawn to the area by its immense beauty and strategic location. In modern times, the small fishing port was transformed into a prestigious resort, made famous in the 1950s by the likes of French film star Bridget Bardot. Like flies on an ice-cream cone, others followed: big Hollywood names, European designers, politicians, artists, royalty and key figures in the global elite. Pretty soon, the sandy beaches and the narrow streets of the old town became crowded with visitors, the locals making room as best they could.

The annual crush started each year in June, when the clear, blue Mediterranean began warming up. Yachts piled up in the elegant port, most arriving from the Caribbean, where their rich owners had been dodging the cold winter weather. Well-heeled visitors hit the shops and beaches, the clubs and restaurants, working hard at relaxation and inevitably showing off. Meanwhile, seasonal workers arrived from France, Italy and Eastern Europe, seeking to make some cash from the whole show.

Gliding through this buzzy, narcissistic scene that hot August afternoon, was a brown Rolls Royce, attended by two black Mercedes saloons and several Peugeots. The locals were quite used to expensive cars, and a Rolls Royce on its own hardly deserved a second glance. However, this particular cortege suggested someone of importance, someone deserving of official French security. Soon there was speculation on the nationality and status of this particular VIP. Could it be Mr Sarkozy and his beautiful wife Carla Bruni? It might be a foreign dignitary on some official visit, they said, but surely not at this time of year? Soon the rumours began to spread: it must be Prince Ali, who had recently been in the media spotlight following the attempt on his life in Nice – and the sad death of his son.

As it turns out, the rumours on this occasion were correct: Ali was heading for his exclusive villa overlooking the spectacular bay. Named La Belle, the place had been created by the crème de la crème of architects and designers from Europe, the United States and the Middle East, ensuring everything was exactly to the prince's taste. For extravagance, there was nothing nearby to top it, with the possible exception of Bill Gates' place in Port Grimaud.

The villa boasted a full complement of staff, ready to serve the prince and his family any time of day or night. Chefs from France and the Middle East worked to produce a tantalizing menu, drawing on the culinary traditions of East and West. Careful of his figure and seeking to make up for the alcohol, Ali would order small portions. He'd always been keen on keeping fit, making the most of the personal gym, staffed by personal trainers. Of course, in the past few years, there had been less incentive to exercise. His sloth, combined with the heavy drinking, had produced a saggy layer of fat over his abdomen.

One facility that was never underused was the bar, with its huge range of drinks, from Cristal Champagne to the humble arak of his native Middle East, not to mention all the beers known to mankind. Whenever the need arose, Ali suppressed his appetite with a few lines of cocaine.

Since the Arab Spring, Ali had had little time to enjoy his luxurious villa in Saint-Tropez. At first, he'd been battling to maintain control of his country. But when that fight was lost, he'd fled to Dubai, then hopped around the world's capital cities, seeking to secure whatever remained of his wealth and power. Now, two months after the death of his beloved son, the prince was returning to his fabulous home-from-home, hoping to rest and recuperate – and to ponder the shattered remains of his life.

The French authorities had been kind enough to secure transport from Nice, the scene of the tragic incident. With the funeral out of the way and Ali's injuries healed, a helicopter had been laid on, with the compliments of the French tax payer. The bodyguards had huddled around him through the whole journey, like mothers protecting their infant. Now, as the Rolls sped along, Ali was struck by the rays of the sun reflecting off the sparkling sea, and he suddenly had the feeling of coming home.

He recalled his childhood, when he'd played more freely, unaware of the demands of the future. Those were the days before his grandfather had seized the throne, pushing aside a distant cousin; Ali was still considered minor royalty, nobody of particular importance. He had enjoyed playing in the sand dunes, even in the scorching heat of August, when the temperature rarely dipped below 45 degrees Celsius. Being by the sea, of course, the humidity had been suffocating – but the young Ali had been quite content, plunging in for a swim whenever possible.

Without warning, the childhood scenes vanished, and he was confronted once more by the insistent images of disaster: the gunshots, the blood, the death of his beloved Shehab, his burial in Nice, the grief and the endless tears.

The car snaked up the steep, winding roads of Ramatuelle. Finally, the cortege pulled up at La Belle, drivers and security guards eager to deliver their precious cargo. As he stepped from the Rolls, he realised how much he'd missed the place; perhaps, at last, he might find some rest, some solace.

According to tradition, he was greeted by the servants, lining up for his reception, gratefully accepting their generous tips from the master. Ali entered the house and headed for the living room. The housekeeper was a middle-aged French lady from Lyon who was glad of such a well-paid job. She was not quite sure whether to welcome the prince back or offer her condolences on his loss. Instead, she asked if he would like to have something to eat. Ali ignored her, walked to the bar, grabbed a bottle of vodka and headed to his bedroom.

On arrival, he was blinded by the bright sun rays pouring through the clean windows. He stood and contemplated the eternal sea, which seemed somehow linked in his mind to the hereafter – the infinity and mystery of the hereafter. What was after death?

He lay on the sofa, sipping at the vodka. He was trying to drown out the noises in his head: the sounds of the attack and the calls of his dead son. Also the endlessly repeated questions: Who wants me dead, and why?

When he opened his eyes, the room was dark. For a moment, he had forgotten where he was. Then it all flooded back, and he rose slowly to his feet. He dragged himself to the bathroom, the latest in modern chic, with its black marble and gilded taps.

He undressed, stepped into the bath and ran the cold tap. He closed his eyes and felt the icy water creeping up slowly, covering him limbs and body. The cold was reviving him somehow, soothing his aches and pains – but nothing could stop the waves of melancholic thought.

He wanted some whirlpool to drag him down, to drown him in the depths of the sea. No matter how hard he tried, he could not find the answer to his eternal question: what was the purpose of his life? The obvious answer returned again and again: there was no purpose to his life, no reason to continue – and he would do best to end it.

He gazed at the electric socket on the wall. He might plug in the hairdryer and drop it into the bath. That would do the job. There was the hairdryer, sitting on the shelf; it would be easy to accomplish. Just a matter of seconds, and all his troubles would be over.

Suddenly, he heard his mother's voice in stereo, scolding him for having such thoughts.

'God will punish you in Hell, my boy,' she said. 'You will upset your beloved son.'

Ali obeyed his mother, rising from the water and stepping slowly from the bath, moving his 48-year-old body like it was 80. Another near-miss, he thought. He should be grateful to be alive, if not for himself, then for the sake of his children and family. He towelled his body dry, glad for once to be doing something without the aid of servants. At school – Eton and Rolle – he had been more independent, doing pretty much everything for himself. And those had been the happiest days of his life, his last days of freedom.

He pulled on a bath robe and wandered back to the bedroom. As he did so, his thoughts drifted back two months to the attempt on his life – scenes from the incident, the hospital and the funeral. He still hadn't properly grieved for his son. In Islamic law, the dead should be buried soon after death. However, due to his own injuries – concussion, broken ribs, deep lacerations – Ali had been unable to negotiate the return of his son's body to his birthplace. Instead, a cousin in Paris – another fugitive from the new regime – had arranged Shehab's burial in Nice, laying him to rest in the Islamic cemetery. As the son's corpse was slid into place, the father lay in hospital, doped up on drugs. When he finally found the physical strength to leave his bed, Ali couldn't quite make it to the tomb, collapsing instead at the cemetery gates.

He woke up in his bedroom, stretched full length on the sofa, agitated and shaky. In a state such as this, nothing but quality vodka could dampen his sorrow, the feelings of loss and guilt. Yes, he would have some more booze and drown his sorrows.

Ali was startled by the phone. He struggled to reach the mobile, pressing the wrong buttons. It took a while to recognize the name of the caller. Then it came to him: it was Omar, French-born, of Tunisian heritage. His parents had fled their country in 1956, after independence from France, seeking a better life for their three children.

Omar worked in the hospitality business, serving the well-off Middle Eastern tourists, catering for their various needs – interpreting, shopping and seeing that the appetites of hungry men were satisfied. Despite the tragedy of Ali's loss, Omar could not quite disguise his cheerful mood. And yet, he was hesitant, not sure what to say. Should he welcome the prince back or offer condolences?

Ali provided the answer, his voice shaky but eager: 'I want to party tonight in Saint-Tropez.'

Omar could not hide his surprise, answering with hesitation: 'Yes, Your Highness. There is no better place than the VIP Room. It is often difficult to get in to, but you're a special case.'

'Well, that's no problem. We will stuff them with gold,' said Ali indifferently, his voice slurred. 'Where are you?'

'I'm not far away, in Toulouse. I can be with you this evening,' said Omar. 'I'll book a table in the private part area, Your Highness. You adored the one in Monaco.'

Ali ignored Omar and allowed his thoughts to wander, planning how he'd deal with his pain by relying on alcohol, sex or clubbing – perhaps all three. Yes, that's what he'd do.

He composed himself and – preparing his booze-sodden throat for a polished French accent – answered harshly: '*D'accord. À onze heures.*'

He hung up without saying goodbye, then rang the bell for service. There was a slight delay before the housekeeper appeared, hurrying into the room.

'*Votre Altesse,*' she said, somewhat flustered.

'Ask the chauffeur to get the car ready. And where is my stylist?'

The poor woman was terrified, informing him in a rather shaky voice that the finance ministry has suspended such unnecessary expenses as grooming the prince. To her amazement, Ali dismissed her without further questioning.

Ali had not lost his sense of elegance and glamour. He remembered his days at Eton, also at Harvard, when he used to dress himself with no help from stylists. This was especially the case in Europe; yes, dressing alone was quite doable.

That said, he had been busy these past few years, not really part of the party scene, and therefore not sure what passed for fashionable these days. Maybe the smart-casual look would do the trick? He pulled out a blue Armani jacket. As for shirts, he selected something yellow from English shirt-maker Thomas Pink. English shirts were his favorite, and this one had been tailored to his increasingly bloated figure and slightly protruding belly. He was certainly fond of those roomy Armani cuts.

He heaved himself into the trousers and pulled up the zip; it was a real struggle and took several attempts. Obviously, he had gained some weight. How much simpler is was to pull on the traditional white robes of his homeland.

He found his way to the bell and pressed the button with a shaky hand. The housekeeper entered, bowing as if in a royal court: '*Oui, Votre Altesse. À votre service.*'

'*Je voudrais aller au VIP Room,*' said the prince.

Omar arrived at the villa in good time. He opened the door of the silver Bentley, which had been designed especially for Ali, who slid into the brown-leather seat, breathing in the scent of luxury. The car sped along the resort's main road, which had transformed since the daytime. Gone were the sun-worshippers in skimpy clothing; now the place looked more sophisticated, bedecked with coloured lights, desperately seeking to compete with Paris.

The car pulled up at the nightclub, close by the marina at the Port de Saint-Tropez. Ali cheered up on seeing the army of waiters attending his arrival, and particularly the manager, who had cut his holidays short to greet him. Omar had booked a big section of the private area. However, first Ali insisted on mingling with the masses. After all, he viewed himself as royalty – but royalty with more freedom than most.

All eyes were on the prince as he moved through the crowd. Young men, some in business suits, others in smart-casual, watched him pass by. The women eyed him up, some lusting after what remained of his good looks, others keen on his fortune and hoping for a small slice of the cake. He was known to be generous with the ladies.

His expert eyes scanned the scene. Here was one woman boasting a trashy look: a strapless, pink-sequinned mini-dress, complete with six-inch, open-toed platforms; hair teased into a high beehive; heavy make-up with black, smoky eyes and bright-pink, glossy lips. She smacked her gum a lot too.

Ali turned his head – away from Omar's protective presence – and was mesmerized by another woman with an altogether more classy look. She was wearing a black, lacy dress that just covered the knees, while her slender legs ran down to sharp-toed high-heels. Here was something elegant. The blond hair was shoulder-length and straight, lending her a more serious look, while the make-up was nicely done. She carried a designer bag, and the watch on her slender wrist seemed expensive. Held delicately in her finely manicured fingers was a Bohemia Crystal glass, from which she sipped Champagne.

She appeared to be no different from any other women in her upper-class social bracket. And yet, Ali could not keep his eyes off her. Despite the relentless attempts of other women to attract his attention, his eyes remained fixed on her face and her cleavage, the movements of her hands and lips.

The prince had never been so drawn to another person. He recalled his love affair with a waitress while he was at university. He used to chase her, slipping away from his entourage, who had been instructed to watch him like hawks. That was indeed a powerful attraction, but this seemed even more so.

Omar had noticed the intensity of the prince's interest, and he took careful note. He whispered discreetly in Ali's ear then approached the woman. She was chatting to a bunch of middle-aged, grey-haired men. They were in their late 40s with a few wrinkles, but they had managed to maintain trim figures, despite all the Champagne.

Omar invited the group to the prince's table. As important businessmen always on the lookout for a good deal, it was an invitation they could hardly refuse. The woman was not very impressed with the move, but she went along with the rest of the group.

They seated themselves comfortably, and Omar made sure that Ali was within reach of the beautiful lady. Ali ordered the best Champagne on the menu, as well as caviar, straight from the Caspian Sea. Omar made a brief introduction and left them to it.

'My name is Ali,' said the prince, speaking with a hint of hesitation.

'I'm Laura,' she answered, avoiding eye contact.

Ali glanced at his prey: such a pretty girl, with her deep-blue eyes and luscious hair. Yes, she certainly stirred something in him: desire, lust, passion, attraction – call it what you will.

He persisted with the dialogue: 'It's very nice to meet you. Are you American?'

'Yes, from New York.'

'I couldn't miss the American accent,' he responded calmly.

'You must watch Hollywood films then?' the woman shot back, her tone clearly sarcastic.

'No, I do not have the time. I studied in the States.'

'I thought you studied in England.'

'I studied there too. My father wanted me to become acquainted with the American system and mentality.'

'And did you?' said the woman.

'I thought so until recently. You may give me a lesson,' said Ali, launching into flirtation mode.

'And what do you mean by that?' she replied, apparently shocked. 'I'm a respectable woman. I'm not going to be added to your list of adventures.'

There was both anger and humiliation in her voice.

'I'm so sorry,' said the prince. 'I did not mean to offend you.'

Omar had overheard the conversation and, picking up on the tension, wondered if he should intervene.

The woman hastily drained her glass and looked around at her companions, asking if the might be ready to move on. The response did not meet her expectations. The gentlemen were happy to be wined and dined by an Arab prince.

Quite unexpectedly, Ali excused himself from the table. Turning to the woman, he said courteously: 'I never intended to upset you.'

He kissed her hand and left. He gestured to his entourage to follow him, instructing them to pay the bill for the table.

Laura felt embarrassed, sorry for having been unnecessarily rude. She knew very well who Ali was, and somehow the thought of being added to the long list of his very public conquests had set her on edge. Even so, she reflected, there was no reason to be so harsh.

She glanced at her remaining male companions and reflected on their lack of gallantry. Not one of them had sided with her when she'd suggested leaving. So much for being a gentleman.

Before long, the Bentley was speeding through Saint-Tropez, heading for the villa. Ali had not felt like this for a very long time; Laura's voice, breath and general appearance seemed to arouse deep emotions within him. Lust, yes – but more besides.

'I want you to get some information about her,' he said.

Omar gulped and cleared his throat: 'At your service, Your Highness.'

The car sped onwards, breaking the speed limit. The speed-camera flashed as the car whizzed along the promenade, blinding the birds as they sat in the trees waiting for sleep.

Chapter 4
The Heat of the Desert

Late summer in Jawhar was blistering. The wind whipped up the sand and hurled it about; it would stick to a face like an egg on a frying pan. Anyone with any sense was hibernating, taking a siesta. In the more affluent cities, that meant taking shelter indoors, where the air-conditioning belted out cool air. However, in the smaller towns and villages across the emirate, such comforts were less common. One was lucky to find shade and a creaky fan.

At 17 years old, Abdul was still a boy. However, in his Bedouin culture, he was considered a man, particularly since the death of his father. He was the eldest of five siblings, each of them separated by just one year, and his mother struggled to feed so many mouths.

The Bedouins felt allegiance only to their family and tribe, disdaining government authorities and their artificial borders. They viewed the desert as their own vast country, largely ignoring the maps drawn up by Western powers since the First World War. For many centuries, they had lived by way of trade and travel, with camels at the centre of their existence.

However, the changes of the modern world had rendered their lifestyle unsustainable. Their traditional, cross-border sources of income had vanished. The camels were replaced with four-by-four Chevrolets and Italian caravans, and governments imposed programmes of settlement. But those programmes had largely failed – and no alternative solutions had been forthcoming.

Residing on the fringes of society and with little access to the national economy, the average family income was meagre. Abdul's family lived just below the poverty line, despite the emirate's relative affluence and the abundant black gold on which it was based.

Abdul's school was 20 miles from his village. He tried to attend regularly, but he couldn't always manage the daily commute in the oven-like heat. With no proper means of transport and summer temperatures around 50 degrees Celsius, it was too much in the end. It didn't help that he had several hungry brothers and sisters to feed, not to mention the burden of being head of the family.

His only indulgence was the time he spent at the local tin-roofed mosque, a peaceful refuge from daily life. Here he would socialize with other youths who lacked a sense of belonging and had all but given up on life. As a habitual truant from school, he lacked the education necessary to understand the intricate language of the Quran. However, he learned to recite the text by heart, following that age-old tradition of memorization. In time, he came to rely on the imam, who would offer his own interpretations of Islam, and he would listen to fatwas – those religious rulings on life designed to distinguish right from wrong.

In time, Abdul became more devoutly religious, praying more than five times each day, his life revolving around the mosque and its attendees. His every move was watched by the quick-tempered imam, who made sure he followed the teachings of Islam faithfully.

Another man was there to help Abdul along the path, a mentor of sorts. This was Idris, in his early 30s, of medium build and a bit on the chubby side. In addition to Islam, Idris relied on food to cope with his frustrations. This made more sense, of course, for an unmarried Muslim man unable to indulge his sexual desires or fall back on mind-altering substances.

Idris had no trade to speak of, normally scratching a living from unskilled labour, and even that was pretty rare. Otherwise, he relied heavily on the imam to provide for his family. Then, at some point, things changed, and Idris was seen wearing new clothes, including expensive *abayas* of black silk. He said a distant relative of his had made good in America – the land of milk and honey – and was now supporting his family.

Around this time, he also began to focus more attention on Abdul's adherence to religious doctrine. He told Abdul not do deviate from the original teachings in the early days of Islam, the time of the Prophet Mohamed, since these represented the true path. Unable to read the Quran for himself, Abdul listened carefully to his mentor's words, viewing him now as a master worthy of obedience and respect. Indeed, he felt that he would do anything for Idris, including sacrificing his life for the sake of Islam.

Abdul was not alone in being brainwashed. Several of his friends from school were also attending the mosque, and they were also sucked into the ideology espoused by Idris. They were easy pickings: teenage boys full of testosterone and lacking any other outlet for their frustration and hopelessness. Abdul and his friends dreamed of the beautiful virgin women and the rivers of wine promised to the martyrs on reaching heaven. Altogether, it was the perfect recipe for disaster.

Idris spoke of the corruption of the West, which leant its support to the corrupt local regimes. He fed these toxic feelings to the boys in his care at every opportunity. As things stood, they were nothing, but they might become something, assuming they followed the correct path.

And so Abdul entered the world of *jihad*, taking as his passport that combination of a sturdy build, loyalty and commitment to the cause laid out by Idris. The boy continued his daily prayers, being the first to enter the mosque each day and the last to leave it, locking the door behind him. He managed to re-channel his disillusion, frustration and feeling of injustice by way of Islamic studies. He would recite the

Quran and listen to Idris provide his own account of Islamic history, including the life of the Prophet Mohamed and his followers in the early days of Islam. Idris tried to re-shape Abdul's peaceful personality, transforming him into an aggressive, rebellious man driven by injustice and frustration, on a mission to reform the world. It was not a very difficult task.

Abdul was also introduced to several older men at the mosque who had experienced *jihad* back in the 1970s, fighting the communists in Afghanistan with American support. They said they had been betrayed and abandoned by the West, which had failed to deliver on its promises. Now they were seeking to assert their own vision of the future. And they had backers in the region willing to make it happen.

Soon Idris was giving Abdul odd jobs around the mosque, providing him with a basic monthly wage and the occasional bonus. Abdul felt things were finally coming together, and it was good to be able to put food on the family table. He felt the respect and gratitude of his mother and sisters. For once, he felt like a real man.

'I feel like I could conquer the world,' he declared one day.

'Yes, I'm sure you could,' said Idris.

Chapter 5
Lac Léman

The shoreline of Lac Léman – better known to visitors as Lake Geneva – is dotted with villas and châteaux. Among the most prized retreats in Europe, these buildings benefit from both beautiful natural scenery and the proximity of a lively, cosmopolitan city.

Many years before, Ali had purchased one such home, a stunning château of Belle Époque design. It had been a present to his second wife, Hasina, who was the daughter of a prominent sheikh. The marriage had been arranged by Ali's family in order to protect their political interests. Hasina's father had sought to unseat Ali's father by way of a coup d'état, and it was only through much conspiring and negotiation that the power struggle had been resolved in favour of Ali's family. The marriage had been a key part of the deal; love hardly came into it.

Ali and Hasina had rarely visited their Swiss property, leaving the servants to enjoy the plush furnishings and serene lakeside setting. Now, after many years, Ali was finally putting in an appearance. Saint-Tropez had worn thin in the end, quite failing to sooth his grief and quiet his racing thoughts. As autumn set in, the prince had turned his attention to Switzerland. Perhaps the serenity of the lake and the cool mountain air would help?

He had been at Lac Léman for two days now, and much of that time had been spent on the sofa, glued to the news and drinking heavily. The situation back home was worrying. The recently established dummy parliament continued to portray him as a monster, providing the people with an easy target for their anger. If the nation's dire economic state and the poverty of the ordinary people could be blamed on Ali, then those who remained might escape responsibility.

He had been officially stripped of his royal title and declared an enemy of the people. Investigations into financial corruption were ongoing. Some parliamentarians had gone so far as to accuse Ali of treason, demanding that he be put on trial – a worrying development indeed.

Ali sat in the vast, gloomy living room, the wide-screen TV flickering away, vodka in hand. Once more, his thoughts began to race; he was sunk in darkness, trapped like a rat in a maze. Suddenly, in the midst of his painful thoughts, there was a feeling a joy, a flash of light amid the darkness. It was a memory of the American woman from the nightclub in Saint-Tropez. Something about the encounter had been soothing, uplifting. Just the mental image of her face brought him a sense of relief.

What was the woman's name?

He grabbed his mobile phone, flipping open the diamond-studded case. He flicked through the smartphone apps and quickly became confused; where were his assistants when he needed them? He scrolled impatiently through the address book, searching in vain for a familiar name. He wasn't even sure he'd taken her number.

Finally, he gave up and clicked on 'Omar, France'. If anyone would know, it was Omar.

'*Bonjour, Votre Altess*,' said Omar in his thick provincial accent.

Ali replied in classical Arabic, his voice sullen: 'I am not a Royal Highness any more. Have you heard the news today?'

'Which news, Your High...?'

Omar swallowed his words.

'Parliament has stripped me of my title, and God knows what's next.'

'Don't give up. Your people love you.'

Ali found no comfort in Omar's reassurances. In fact, he wanted to cut the crap, forget the sweet talk. There were more pressing matters at hand.

'Listen, do you remember the girl we met at that night club in Saint-Tropez?'

'Do you mean in the VIP Room?'

'That's right.'

'Yes, Laura. What about her?'

'I want to see her,' said Ali, his princely authority asserting itself.

Omar began to speak, but his shaky voice couldn't quite form the words. Ali, who was already irritated, became suddenly more so.

'What is the problem? Spit it out!'

'Well, your highness, Laura is not free,' Omar replied worriedly.

'Is she married?' Ali asked.

'No, Your Highness. She is with Monsieur Vallois, the wealthy French industrialist.'

'Well, I am Prince Ali, the ...'

Ali stopped mid-sentence, reflecting on his lack of both title and power, not to mention the likely scarcity of money in the future.

Omar knew that it would be extremely difficult to persuade Laura to cancel on Monsieur Vallois and see Ali instead. However, he also knew that Ali did not generally take no for an answer.

Taking note of Omar's hesitation, Ali resorted to his standard position, which was to pay whatever sum was necessary to get the job done.

'Fine,' he said, 'do whatever is necessary. I will pay all expenses.'

'Yes, of course,' said Omar. 'I will contact her immediately.'

Ali hung up and sank back into the sofa. His body was aching horribly, as was his head. The previous night's prolonged drinking session had left him with a serious hangover. He'd wandered aimlessly from one bar to another, with alcohol as his sole reliable companion. In one bar he posed as a tourist, in another as a refugee. He recalled visiting L'Atelier Cocktail Club, but the rest was rather hazy. Indeed, he had no recollection of arriving home. Presumably, the chauffeur had taken care of all that.

The TV flickered and his thoughts followed their usual routes: home, politics, family, his beloved son. Once again, Laura popped into his mind, and along with her phantasmal presence came a sensation of joy, of brightness – the hint of tender sentiments that he had not felt for a very long time.

Laura reminded him of his first love, Jomana, the daughter of an employee in the royal household. For a brief period, she was the love of his life and meant the world to him. Keen to exercise his muscularity, Ali had taken her virginity. Of course, marrying the girl was out of the question, and when Ali's father discovered the love affair, he dismissed Jomana's father from his service. The man was paid a handsome sum by way of compensation, and Ali tried to save the situation by arranging a small operation abroad to restore Jomana's virginity. She disappeared from his radar, and then some time later he learned that she had taken her life, unable to live with the shame she had brought upon her family.

Since that time, Jomana's ghost had often visited Ali at night, entering his dreams, silently reminding him of his actions and arousing remorse.

Now Laura was tugging at his heart strings, reminding him of the possibility of love. He was haunted by her beauty and the scent of her perfume. It seemed the only way to deal with this curse was to make love to the woman, and thereby determine finally whether it was just lust – or something else.

The latest news from Jawhar was not good. The TV was showing the aftermath of explosions in the capital city, dead bodies littering the downtown area. There were also demonstrations demanding reforms. Ali found the whole thing rather ironic.

'I have left Jawhar and am being branded as a devil – but in my absence, the country is in turmoil.'

He thought of his remaining children, still in the country of their birth, sheltering with relatives while the place went up in flames. Were they safe?

He picked up the phone, and with a trembling hand began to dial. At first, he got a wrong number, then he got through to his cousin and confidant, Sheikh Hassan.

'*Salaam*,' said Ali, his voice wavering.

'*As-Salaamu Alaikum*,' replied Hassan, his voice oozing confidence.

Ali was reassured by the greeting, a sign that one person at least was honest enough to maintain friendly relations with him, despite his fallen state.

'I miss you,' said Ali, bursting into tears.

'Me too, my cousin.'

Hassan had renounced both politics and life's hedonistic pleasures. As a practicing Muslim of moderate views, he disagreed with Ali's lifestyle. Nevertheless, he had been a rock to Ali, providing support when his father died. The father was famed for his cruelty in dealing with his people, his children and his wives, but his passing had been a difficult time for the prince.

Hassan listened to his cousin's pitiful, drunken sobs, waiting for the chance to speak.

'Ali, your family is fine,' he said at last. There was a moment of silence. Then he continued: 'Please try not to call again.'

Ali panicked: 'Why Hassan? What have I done?'

'Nothing,' said Hassan, 'but the situation is vile. We do not need more problems. It's in everyone's best interests.'

Ali hung up the phone and sobbed more heavily than ever. He had never imagined that his family would disown him for the sake of their own safety. His sense of isolation was complete. He staggered to the bedroom and slumped down on the slippery silk sheets. He lay on his back, gazing into the darkness. His body felt strangely numb, as if he were drifting, slipping through the dark, silky air.

Whatever would happen next? He had lost his country, his throne and his family. Whatever was next? Could things possibly get any worse?

He awoke to the harsh sound of the telephone. On the other end was Omar.

'Forgive me, Your Highness.'

'Yes,' said Ali, rather croakily, not sure yet what language he was hearing.

'This is Omar, Your Highness.'

'Yes, go ahead.'

'I have traced Laura. She is in Zurich.'

The woman's name jolted Ali fully awake.

'Where is she? I want to see her.'

'I managed to locate her and she is very keen to meet you.'

Omar's tone was stronger now. He had sensed the power that Laura's name had over the prince, and he felt that some of that power now rested in him, as middle-man.

'There's something, Your Highness, that I want to tell you. But I'm a bit afraid of how you'll take it.'

'Spit it out, Omar! Is she committed to this bloody French guy? If so, I will pay him. I'll pay whatever is necessary.'

'No, Your Highness, I'm afraid you will have to pay her instead.'

'What are you saying?' barked Ali at full volume. 'Are you saying she is a prostitute?'

Omar held the phone away from his ear, fearful of an angry outburst.

'Yes sir,' he said at last, wondering if this might be his last job with this particular client.

But Omar need not have worried, for Ali, being a man of experience, had already factored in this very possibility. He was annoyed, for sure, but not entirely surprised.

''So what? I still want to see her. I didn't think that she was Lady Diana.'

'No, Your Highness.'

'Pay her whatever she wants. I will devote an open budget to this.'

'Yes, Your Highness.'

Ali hung up the phone.

He lay in the gloom and pondered the possibility of downing another drink. He reflected, not for the first time, that drinking alcohol was a sin, at least according to his faith. His mother's voice could be heard, imploring him to repent.

Brushing these obstacles aside, he marched to the living-room bar and poured a large martini, gulping it down greedily. The prospect of meeting Laura again seemed to have aroused a mix of excitement and nerves. He would need steady nerves for this one. After all, it wasn't every day that one stumbled upon the Holy Grail.

His stomach rumbled; he hadn't eaten since the night before. He grabbed a handful of pistachios and walnuts and started munching. As the booze entered his bloodstream and the nuts reached his stomach, he began to feel quite revived.

'I will regain my throne, save my people and even make love to Laura!' he declared.

And he poured another martini.

* * *

Ali awoke the next morning to the sound of the maid's heels on the marble floor. She was trying her best to be quiet, but there was really nothing for it. The housekeeper had sent her to rouse the master from his sleep. Ali had spent the night on the enormous sofa, the TV flickering silently.

'Excuse me, Your Highness,' said the young maid, terrified of the consequences of waking her drink-sodden employer before he was good and ready.

Ali opened an eye: 'Yes, what is it?'

'A gentleman named Omar is here,' explained the maid. 'He's causing a terrible row outside. He's demanding to see Your Highness immediately. What should be done?'

'It's quite alright,' said Ali. 'Just start my bath running.'

'Right away,' said the maid, delighted at such a manageable instruction. And she skipped off to the bathroom.

Without warning, Omar burst into the living room, stopping some yards from the sofa to offer a bow. A male servant hovered nervously in the doorway.

'Good morning, Your Highness,' said Omar.

Ali yawned, placing a hand over his mouth and smoothing his well-groomed moustache.

'What's the latest?'

'It's all taken care of. After some considerable effort, I have managed to locate Laura.'

Omar hoped that by emphasizing the difficulty of the task, he might obtain a bigger tip.

'Where is she? When shall I see her?'

'I will arrange a meeting at the Four Seasons Hotel.'

Ali dragged himself from the luxury sofa.

'Book the Royal Suite,' he said.

With the measured movements of a man in his late forties, Ali made his way to the bathroom, where he found the bath filling nicely and full of bubbles. He wiped the steam from the mirror. The face that stared back at him was quite a shock: there were new wrinkles, and his famous hazel eyes were circled in black. Those very eyes had once been like magnets to the girls who bought the paparazzi magazines just to fantasise about spending a private moment with him.

He searched through the moisturisers and anti-wrinkle creams; one of these famous French brands would surely do the trick. Or perhaps he had time for a Botox injection? Alas, there was no time. The woman who had put a sparkle in his heart would just have to take him as he was.

With no further ado, he plunged into the bath, complete with flower-scented bubbles. Such a delicious experience; only the thought of meeting Laura could drag him away. Properly washed and scented, he rushed to his wardrobe and picked out a casual suit, dark olive to compliment his skin color. He was becoming quite accustomed to life without a personal dresser.

'Tell the chauffeur to prepare the Jaguar,' he told the housekeeper.

The car sped along the lake shore, gliding through calm neighbourhoods populated by the rich and famous. They had come here for the natural beauty, the sophisticated culture and the tax regime designed to make wealthy foreigners feel at home. Finally, the Jaguar rolled up to the hotel, stationed on the Quai des Bergues, overlooking the Pont du Mont-Blanc and L'île Rousseau. The Four Seasons, owned by the fourth generation of the same family, boasted six stars. At the entrance stood an array of staff members, ready to help new arrivals and take a generous tip in the process.

Ali was on automatic pilot, ignoring the greetings as he passed through the main entrance. He headed straight to the bar, where his special-blend whisky was waiting for him. He sank back into a chair, took a large sip, and stared into space.

The tranquility was broken by Omar rushing in, apparently in a panic.

'What's up?' Ali murmured.

'I'm sorry, Your Highness. There's a problem.'

'Well, what is it? Spit it out!'

'Well, sir, Laura has refused to come.'

Ali threw the crystal tumbler on the floor. Luckily, the thick rug cushioned the fall.

'Who does she think she is? Pay her whatever she asks. She's just a prostitute, after all.'

'I've tried that, sir, with no luck.'

'What do you mean?'

Ali was shouting now. His pride was wounded, and in true form, he'd resorted to anger.

'Well,' said Omar, picking his words carefully, 'she has dared to ask Your Highness to meet her at the Crazy Horse bar.'

Ali shot to his feet, his face red with fury.

'Okay, we shall see what happens to someone who disobeys Ali bin Kased!'

He stormed out of the bar and through the lobby, scattering the assembled staff, who were terrified that the prince might have been unhappy with the service. Too furious to wait for his car, Ali got into a taxi by the main gate.

'To the Crazy Horse!' he shouted.

As the poor driver sped through the narrow city streets, Ali realised that he was taking his very first taxi ride – and without the help of a servant. He knew the name of the bar, but he had no idea of the address; he had simply to trust the driver's local knowledge. Finally, the vehicle came to a halt by the train station. And there was the bar, as if by magic.

Ali leaped out and made for the entrance, only to hear the driver calling after him, demanding to be paid. Moments later, a second taxi came to a screeching halt, and Omar emerged at high speed, paying both drivers, complete with hefty tip.

Ali entered the bar, still in a foul mood. He stood in the middle of the room and looked around. Where on earth was the woman? He realised suddenly that his recollection of Laura's face was rather vague. He knew that she was very pretty, articulate, attractive, like so many of the models and actresses he'd dated in the past. But the details of her face were a little hazy. His eyes scanned the small room: a few people on stools by the bar itself, the rest dotted among the simple tables. No Laura, apparently.

He sat on a sofa and ordered a large vodka and Coke. Several businessmen nearby were chatting up a group of North African girls, flirting gaily in French. One of the girls came and tried it on with Ali, but she was waved away without ceremony. How humiliating, he thought, to be approached by a cheap prostitute in a common bar. Had he really fallen so far?

He necked his drink and ordered another. He watched and waited, and he drank some more. He seemed to recall this particular bar having a seedy reputation. Perhaps this was a wild goose chase, the stupid woman's idea of a joke.

At the far end of the room, a heavy door swung open and a young blonde woman walked in. She wore a simple blue top, rose-coloured trousers and high heels. The make-up was minimal: dark eyeliner round her big, blue eyes and light lipstick to match the trousers. She looked like an ordinary – though very pretty – office girl seeking to unwind after the hassle of a working day.

Ali eyed her intensely. Was this the same girl? Was this Laura?

She walked up confidently and greeted him in French, her American accent quite evident.

'Bonsoir, monsieur.'

Ali looked around quickly to be sure she hadn't mistaken him for someone else.

'Bonsoir, madame,' he replied.

'I'm Laura. Are you Ali?'

'Yes, I am.'

He picked up the East Coast in her accent, and combined with her assertive tone, he found the whole package very appealing. He got to his feet and offered his hand. He was not in the habit of rising to greet women – with the possible exception of his mother and visiting diplomats and royals. They shook hands and he invited her to a seat on the sofa.

'We met in Saint-Tropez, I guess,' she said quietly.

'Yes, we did.'

'Well, it's a pleasure to meet you again, Your Highness.'

'Let's drop the titles, please,' he said, 'I am not even a prince anymore. My name is Ali, plain and simple. If you feel more comfortable, you can call me Al.'

The waitress handed them the drinks menu. Ali ordered a vintage whisky from 1940; Laura went for a mojito, that Cuban cocktail so popular in the swanky bars of New York. Suddenly, Ali realised that his fury had vanished. Indeed, he was quite calm, apparently soothed by the physical presence of this beautiful woman.

Anyway, he had no need to be nervous. The situation was hardly new for a prince used to bedding high-class escort girls. He had ordered them over the phone, picked them out from catalogues, and occasionally met them in nightclubs. In each case, it was a business transaction of a purely physical nature, highly confidential, applying the standard code of secrecy.

However, this time something was different. Here he was in a public place, a place of the woman's choosing. They were playing by her rules, and he was going along with it. As he watched her sip her drink, a strange feeling overwhelmed him. It was the same feeling he'd had with his first love, with Jomana – an intense, sincere passion, reckless and joyful.

In light of such feelings, his former sorrows seemed suddenly meaningless. Yes, he had lost his throne and his family, also his beloved son. Yes, he was now slightly less sure of his financial status than before. But what did any of that matter when he had a woman like Laura in his life? The past was dead, gone. Here was the present – the future even – in the living, breathing form of a beautiful woman. And not just dazzling, but strong, intelligent, perhaps even a match for a fallen prince.

What was going on here? Was this mere infatuation or true love? Even in those heady days of his youth, when he courted Jomana, he had not asked himself such questions. Now, however, they seemed of central importance to his existence.

Ali and Laura began to chat, exchanging potted histories of their lives, their backgrounds and current circumstances. The more Laura said, the more Ali wanted to hear. He lapped it up: her childhood, her education, her likes and dislikes. Such interest in the lives of others was quite out of character for the prince, of course, and he made a careful note of this development in his priorities.

Laura, meanwhile, was bewildered. Up to this point, she's known Ali as the playboy prince, famous for his lavish spending; also somewhat reckless and a ruthless ruler. Now she was seeing a new side of the man: courteous, attentive, a good listener. She was in a position to see the human side of the prince that so many had apparently missed, or else refused to acknowledge.

In her line of work, she was used to being treated like a piece of meat by clients – and even worse by the high-society escort agency. She recalled her first job as an escort, while still a student at the University of Montpellier. She was studying for her PhD on the works of Mollier, and funds had run dry. Her middle-class family in New York – two parents in teaching and a younger sister – could not support her any longer, and she needed a solution; she needed lots of cash, and fast. A friend had suggested the escort agency, and Laura had given it a shot. Pretty soon, motivated by the prospect of abject poverty, she had lent her endorsement to the world's oldest profession.

In the following years, she had learnt how to deal with clients: warming up the shy and anxious ones, reaching deals with the abusive ones. Madame Claude, the senior madam at her agency, told her the two secrets of success: 'Never fall in love and never take drugs.'

If she followed these golden rules, Laura would make a great career, said the old woman – and she was right. Laura had never looked back, earning ten times more than most academics in Europe or the US. She was showered with jewellery from

Tiffany and Cartier. All she had to do was provide high-rolling men with some relief – and they were not all bastards. Some were young and handsome; some treated her with delicacy, like a princess; some gave her sexual satisfaction.

Occasionally, there were strange clients, smelling badly or treating her with disrespect. Once in a while, she met a psychopath who might possibly endanger her life. But Laura had become street-wise, spotting the danger miles away, and she knew how to handle them. Her clients come from all walks of life: lawyers, doctors, judges, teachers, businessmen, gangsters, politicians – and finally a prince.

Now, faced with Ali's charms and his seductive hazel eyes, she felt all her tricks and strategies melting away.

Laura recalled her first encounter with the prince: oggling him in the pages of OK magazine when she was a teenager. She recalled one particular evening inspecting his photo closely in the bedroom she shared with her sister. Since then, of course, he had lost some of his youthful good looks; he had become chubbier and sprouted a few grey hairs. But he was still handsome, still Prince Charming, and if anything, the grey hairs seemed to make him more distinguished.

Sitting in the Crazy Horse, she was playing it cool, as she always did with clients. But the truth was that she'd been over the moon when Ali had got in touch. She couldn't believe her luck when Madame Claude had contacted her via Skype to pass on the good news. The old woman was thrilled too, dancing around her apartment in Place Vendôme, Paris, while Laura listened closely.

'Chouchou, this is your chance!' she said. 'He's a prince. This sort of thing only happens once in a lifetime. Don't screw this up!'

Madame Claude was right, of course. It was certainly a once-in-a-lifetime opportunity. Not only would she meet a handsome prince, but one swamped by troubles and in need of support. Perhaps what he needed at this point in his life was a woman to lend a hand, to help him shoulder the burdens. She could certainly do with moving on, putting this sordid profession behind her. At night, men kissed her feet and showered her with money and flowers; the next morning, they sprayed disinfectant everywhere she'd been.

Ali was content to do most of the listening, sipping slowly at his vintage whisky. And while he did so, he examined her every detail: the pretty, round face; the clear skin; the minimalist make-up, which anyway she didn't need. He appreciated her style too: the simple clothing, neat and delicate; the high-heels from Prada, perfectly sculpted to her tiny, well-pedicured feet. He decided she was like a Greek sculpture, perhaps the life-model for a modern-day Venus.

Normally, such women were there to satisfy Ali's desires, plain and simple. With Laura, however, he felt quite different. He would never order her to bed. Much less would he force her into some perverse sex act that she wasn't quite happy with.

Quite out of nowhere, Ali whispered: '*Vous êtes belle, mademoiselle.*'

He lifted her hand from the table and kissed it gently. Laura was surprised by the delicacy of his touch. She did not normally associate rich Arab clients with such tender ways. The fact that he had chosen to compliment her beauty in French simply added to her pleasure.

Ali reached for the Champagne and attempted to pop the cork. He had hoped to impress her with the move, but the cork wouldn't budge. The combination of shaky hands and his over-reliance on English butlers had rendered him rather useless in this department. Somewhat embarrassed, he tried to call the waiter. However, Laura wanted to have a go herself, quite confident in her cork-popping skills.

She grabbed the bottle, and as their hands touched, Ali was taken by surprise. Their eyes met for a brief moment. Who was in control here? Finally, he let go, and Laura's powerful thumbs sent the cork flying. The Champagne spurted forth, and she poured the expensive foam into the glasses.

Ali seemed content with the outcome. He smiled his most charming smile and nodded in appreciation, as if to say: 'So, here we are. It seems you're the boss.'

With no warning, she squeezed her slim body next to his, pressing up against his slightly protruding belly. Their eyes closed and they began to kiss, mouths and tongues moving in perfect harmony, man and woman united, as if they were made for each other, never to be parted. Madame Claude's long-heeded advice about not falling in love was quickly flying out the window. But, as she had said, this was a once-in-a-lifetime event – and the chemistry was shocking.

Ali desperately wanted to ask Laura to the Four Seasons, where the Royal Suite was waiting patiently for them. But it seemed crass to raise the subject in the usual, blunt way. They sipped their drinks, and finally he asked – with great hesitation – whether she was tired. She said that she would certainly enjoy some privacy.

They paid up and left the bar, slipping into the Jaguar and racing to the Four Seasons. Setting aside their usual anxieties about sexual performance, they resolved to simply enjoy the moment. And enjoy it they did.

Chapter 6
Conspiring at The Ritz

There is nothing more breathtaking than a bright spring day in London. The parks are so pretty, with their English roses and huge trees, hinting at the great history of the city, stretching back to Londinium in Roman times. Piccadilly Circus buzzes with life, Eros and his bow suggesting romantic encounters, while nearby, Trafalgar Square, with its stone lions and Nelson's Column, boasts of the British Empire's many victories.

Slightly to the west is the exclusive Mayfair district, with its elegant houses, luxury cars and expensive bars and restaurants. A few blocks south is Buckingham Palace, the London residence of Her Majesty Queen Elizabeth II. Somewhere amidst all this opulence and history is the iconic Ritz Hotel, opened in 1906 by Swiss hotelier Cezar Ritz, whose Paris Ritz was already a hit.

Here, in the hotel's Palm Court, decked out in Louis XVI style, with gilded columns and French chandeliers, a secret meeting was underway. The event was nothing new to a hotel used to hosting heads of state – both current and former, with or without their crowns. As per usual, the dining tables were arranged by experts, trained hoteliers, graduated from the École Hôtelier de Lausanne – the distance between plates and glasses measured with an accuracy bordering on obsession.

On this particular day, there was a scent of expensive perfume in the air, an indication of the high status of the dozen or so guests around the table. Some of the older men were overweight, feeling uncomfortable in their designer suits. The younger ones, meanwhile, were glad to show off their slim figures, complimented by Armani cuts. A few even tried their hand at seducing the pretty young waitresses. Their dark, sun-tanned skin gave a clue to the strength of the sun in their land of origin.

The central figure was also the oldest: a man in his late seventies, keen on displaying his importance and influence, asserting power through age. Nearby sat Ali, and next to him was Razak, a cousin of Ali's father. This close relative was one of several who had disowned Ali since his abdication, seeking to save his own skin. It had been in vain, however, for anyone close to the throne was alienated, scapegoated as a means of absorbing the anger of the people.

Ali had long ago signed a decree stating that he would relinquish his power and sever all ties with Jawhar. In return, he would enjoy a generous allowance and keep his family homes in Europe and the States, thereby allowing him to continue his lavish lifestyle – but based in the West. Since meeting Laura, his life had taken another turn, but it seemed he would never know peace for long. Now these relatives of his, angry at having lost their privileged positions, were pressuring him to reassert his claim to the throne. If Ali returned to his former glory, so would they.

Razak was struggling with his designer suit, his large gut straining his trouser belt. His words were unclear, his mouth full of the finest Ritz pastries and cakes, which had arrived along with the old silver tea set. He was determined, at any price, to get Ali back into power, thereby allowing him to regain his import-export license, with which he had made his millions. He also secretly believed that his own son might have a shot at power, despite his distance from the line of inheritance – if only Ali could be persuaded to return.

Now, seated at the table, he was in full manipulation mode, seeking to convince the other members of his tribe, along with Ali, of the only acceptable course of action.

'Your Highness,' he said, 'your people are dying and are demanding to have you back.'

Ali was quite aware of his distant cousin's motivations as he desperately attempted to canvass the assembled company's support. When he was in power, Ali's intelligence network had kept him informed of Razak's contacts with the Americans, the British and even the Chinese, who showed interest in the natural resources of that small principality. Oil was the vital element that the Chinese needed to operate their giant machinery, as they continued the biggest industrial spurt since Europe's Industrial Revolution two centuries earlier.

Ali was also aware of the rumours that Western powers had masterminded his abdication in part because he had dared to initiate contact with the Chinese without obtaining permission from the West.

Razak picked up on Ali's silence, apparently a sign of inward reflection. He raised his voice politely: 'Your Highness, are you with us?'

Ali gave give him a hard stare, seeking to put him back in his place.

'I'm just wondering what this is all about,' said the prince.

'It's about you, Sir. We are concerned about you and the situation.'

'And your own,' laughed the prince. 'You were one of the first members of my family to betray me and sign the abdication decree. Do you remember?'

Razak tried to clear his throat. His son, who sat by his side, passed him a glass of water.

'Your Highness, I swear to God, they forced me. I was worried about your safety.'

In a gesture that could only be considered an insult, Ali turned away in his seat, showing Razak his back.

'Never mind,' said the prince. 'I forgive you.'

Despite Ali's apparent show of disgust, Razak continued.

'Come back home, master.'

Ali turned and looked into the man's eyes; he saw both fear and the hint of a warning. Here was the relative that Ali had known since his youth, someone he had befriended at an early age – someone he should be able to trust.

'Your Highness,' said Jabber, cutting in, 'your safety is paramount. Yes, we want you back, but on condition that no harm should come to you.'

The statement came like a breath of fresh spring air. Jabber was one of the few people that Ali considered trustworthy, someone who had always kept him informed of corruption within his family and entourage. Nearby was another person Ali had always trusted: his brother-in-law Mahmoud. However, the man's silence on this occasion was worrying.

As Ali pondered his response, others started to offer their own arguments for the prince's return, talking over each other in the rush to explain and persuade. Pretty soon, the chatter round the table had taken on the tone of a loud cocktail party. There was some difference of opinion on minor points; but they were all agreed on the importance of re-instating Ali – and sharing the loot.

Watching the assembled tribal members scrabbling to regain their power and positions, Ali had the feeling of having gambled and lost. Having been lulled somewhat by Jabber's kind words, he now came back down to earth. He cleared his throat and, adopting the confident, alpha-male voice of a television announcer, he began to speak.

'Gentlemen and relatives, I would like to take this opportunity to thank you for your concern and care. I am fine, but Jawhar is not. The priority here is our lovely country, regardless of who is the leader. And if the solution is to have another person in charge, rather than myself, then I will support him.'

His voice was drowned out by the cries of protest, each backed by a strong argument. Chief among them was allegiance to family and tribe. In the eyes of the assembled company, Ali's refusal to at least attempt to retake the throne was an act of betrayal; without him as their figurehead, the chances of the tribe regaining its former status were slim to nothing. Such an act of betrayal would be a stain not only on Ali, but also on his offspring.

All of a sudden, Ali rose from his comfortable chair. With an impulsive gesture, as if propelled by an electric current, he shouted in Arabic: 'Stop! Everyone shut up!'

The unexpected gesture brought an unusual tranquility to that miniature Eastern bazaar in the heart of London. The prince's hands were shaking now, the combined effect of alcohol withdrawal and fear of the unknown.

In a dreamy moment, he stood looking at the assembled crowd, contemplating the prospect of ruling his nation once more, this time with Laura by his side. It would difficult, but she might convert to Islam, making her the legitimate first lady of Jawhar. She might even provide him with an heir.

From within this dreamlike mood, he began to speak: 'My family, brothers and friends. You are the only support I have, the crutch on which I lean.'

He paused, looking around for a glass of water. Instantly, several were offered. Downing some Vichy water, he cleared his throat and continued.

'Our nation is going through hard times. The foreign and neighboring powers will not leave us in peace. It is not only you and me who are the victims of these events. It is mostly the ordinary people who will pay the price.'

Ali raised his head and scanned the large table, seeking to assess their loyalty, just as any dictator might. He locked eyes with Mahmoud, who had gone into exile in Switzerland before the abdication. Mahmoud had married Ali's older sister, Aliya. She was Ali's favourite sibling, someone with sufficient maturity to play the role of mother.

Mahmoud had predicted that the Arab Spring would affect Jawhar sooner or later. He had tried to advocate for reforms, with the support Aliya. But it had all come too late, and the couple had resigned themselves to life in exile. Ali wondered for a moment how differently it might all have turned out.

As he stood thinking, the chatter started up again. Ali was longing for his hotel room and a glass of whisky. He gestured to Mahmoud to accompany him, a move that only provoked jealousy and suspicion among the others, particularly as Mahmoud's influence over the prince was well known.

They left the hall, their departure accompanied by protests of various sorts, including a few slanderous comments. The chauffeur was waiting.

'Where to, sir?'

'The nearest pub,' said the prince, quietly.

As a practicing Muslim, Mahmoud never touched alcohol, and he didn't try to hide his disgust at Ali's suggested destination.

'Can we go to the Arabic café in Harrods?' he suggested.

'You know, my dear cousin, I will be recognized by the clients. And to be frank, I need a drink.'

Mahmoud clasped his hands together in dismay as the car pulled away into the traffic.

'What's going on?' hissed Mahmoud. 'You've been on a mission of self-destruction since you stepped down, perhaps even before that, when the trouble started.'

Ali looked at the floor, not wanting to challenge his brother-in-law, who had always been both direct and insightful in his comments.

'I should have listened to your advice then,' said Ali at last. 'I listened to them instead, and here I am in this current situation.'

Mahmoud wanted to keep talking, but he kept silent. He was aware of the fact that the driver was an Englishman. And as a former interior minister, he was also well aware of the methods of Western intelligence. Even in Arabic, it was not safe to talk further in the car.

Finally, they stopped outside a pub in Mayfair, a suitable venue for a quiet drink. Mahmoud helped Ali out of the car. The prince's body was shaking now, and Mahmoud quietly prayed, asking God to forgive him for being in the company of a consumer of alcohol.

Ali chose a quiet seat at the back, separated from the neighboring tables by a wooden panel. He was in need of some privacy. He ordered his favorite: a double Johnnie Walker on the rocks. Mahmoud refused to drink anything, fearful of traces of alcohol on the pub's glasses. However, after some reassurance from the waitress, he ordered an orange juice.

Mahmoud began to talk about his life in Geneva, about Aliya and their future plans. The Swiss authorities were strict about residency and unwilling to grant them asylum due to the cost of personal protection. He scanned the pub with his careful, brown eyes, the eyes of a former interior minister.

Finally, he turned to Ali, his tone one of reassurance: 'Not to worry. We will get ourselves sorted eventually. What about you? Do you agree with what the family is saying?'

Ali remained silent, looking into his glass.

'You know,' continued Mahmoud, 'Aliya and I worry about you.'

Ali shot him a look of disbelief and downed his whisky in one go. He called the waitress and ordered another one, while Mahmoud looked on in open disgust.

'I said Aliya and I are concerned about you,' Mahmoud insisted.

Ali giggled: 'Tell dear Aliya that I am not a baby any more. I no longer need to be protected from bullies.'

Mahmoud leaned closer and whispered: 'We worry about you now more than ever. There are many things you need to fix. I'm sorry, it's not my intention to lecture you, but your health should be your top priority.'

Ali shot to his feet, enraged, bumping into the table and spilling the orange juice.

'How dare to talk to me like that! I am still the prince, your prince!'

Mahmoud was shocked, almost falling back off his wooden chair. He got to his feet and made for the door. Half way across the room, he turned and looked Ali in the eyes.

'You know, I'm worried that if you continue like this, you're finished,' he said. And he passed smartly into the street.

Ali sat down, gazing into his whisky, his eyes filling with tears.

He heard a voice in his head, castigating him for his actions: 'What I've done is very stupid, unbelievably so. Mahmoud and Aliya were my only friends from the old days. What have I done?'

He took a sip of whisky and pondered his situation some more.

Before long, another voice took over, the voice of a born leader: 'But you are the boss, and they obey you. They are your people, and they need you.'

He took another sip and wondered which voice was more reliable – which version of Ali was more real. Before long, the tears began rolling down his cheeks.

He whipped out his mobile phone and dialled a number.

'Hello. Can I speak to Laura please?'

Chapter 7
The Fugitive

The Knightsbridge area of London is nothing if not glamorous, with its stately Edwardian architecture and high-class superstores, including the world-famous Harrods and Harvey Nichols. It is not only the elites of London who come here for their shopping, but the wealthy from across the globe. Many of those same people have settled in the area too, or at least bought property, snapping up a plush terraced house or perhaps a mansion.

Many years earlier, Ali and his family had acquired an enormous mansion near Belgravia Square. The place oozed with the glamour of its owners, extending to four floors and overlooking a huge garden, which was a rare and highly sought-after thing in the city centre.

It would be hard to count the properties Ali's family had acquired across the world over the years. Even Ali had not kept track, until a gentle reminder from the embassy in London alerted him to the mounting bills from various quarters, all of which must be paid.

The embassy took the opportunity also to mention certain rumours that were circulating in the press, both in Britain and back home. Britain's tabloid press was printing gossip about his lavish lifestyle, along with the dismay that this was causing his fellow countrymen.

In both Western and Arabic newspapers, Ali was depicted as completely reckless, an alcoholic frittering away his fortune. To add insult to injury, Laura, having been exposed to the public gaze by the British press, was depicted in the Arab world as quite evil – an infidel, a Westerner and a prostitute.

For Ali, meanwhile, she was the only source of hope, the one thing that kept him going. He dreamed of her lips, her rosy cheeks and her prominent breasts. A cuddle with Laura was both luxurious and reassuring, unlike anything he'd experienced with his other sexual partners. Tucked away in their London mansion, the couple seemed perfectly happy for a while, and the servants gave them all the space they needed.

However, the Garden of Eden could not last forever. Ali's drinking and subsequent hangovers increasingly undermined his health. Not only was he lackluster and sullen, but his performance in bed was suffering too.

On this particular summer's afternoon, Laura was in a horrible mood, by turns begging and threatening, pleading with him to lay off the booze.

Ali responded with the bruised ego of an alpha male: 'What do you want me to do? There's nothing wrong with me, for God sake!'

'Look how many empty bottles you've made ready for recycling,' said Laura.

Ali struggled to get up from the sofa, gripping the arm like an old man, but he got nowhere fast. He tried to answer back, but he was lost of words. Moments later, his eyes were welling up with tears, a rare thing indeed for a man with long training in the stiff upper lip. Laura rushed over, holding him tightly in her arms.

'Forgive me, darling! I didn't mean it,' she said. 'I just want you to be Ali, the person that everyone knows and loves so much.'

She wiped his tears away with the sleeves of her silk robe. Then she kissed him, her tongue touching his trembling lips. He held her tight and pulled off her robe roughly, demonstrating his muscularity and passion. She showed him her submissive side, making way for his manhood. They rolled over on the bed, and he ended up on top, ready for action.

Just then, the telephone rang.

Ali started swearing in Arabic. He answered abruptly, his voice like thunder. On the other end was the ambassador, both apologetic and remorseful.

'Forgive me, Your Highness. I would not have called you, but it's an emergency and I have to warn you.'

Ali realized his extreme rudeness and shifted to a more reasonable tone.

'What's happened?' he said.

The ambassador's voice was shaking, and as he addressed the deposed head of state, he chose his words carefully.

'British Intelligence have warned us of another attempt on your life. They think that they may not be able to protect you.'

Ali wanted to rubbish his concerns.

'What do they mean? I have a policeman standing at the gate of my property, provided by the British government for my protection.'

As he spoke, he knew that his display of confidence was largely a front. He had been let down by the French, and the Swiss had refused to provide protection, although they had been very apologetic about it. Perhaps the British were about to fail him too.

The ambassador's voice took on a more candid tone: 'Well, Your Highness, they expressed their concerns, and also said they wished to avoid any problems with the new rulers of Jawhar.'

Ali got the message straight away; no further explanation required. He was not welcome in Britain any longer and must leave soon – or face death at the hands of assassins.

He dropped the telephone, leaving a confused ambassador shouting: 'Your Highness! Are you there?'

Laura picked up the mobile from the Kashan Persian carpet.

'I'm sorry, he's busy. He'll call back later,' she said, hanging up.

In one soft and rapid move she took Ali in her arms, as if gathering up the shattered pieces of the man. She kissed him and their tears mixed together.

Chapter 8
The Chaos

The economy in Jawhar had been seriously battered by the events of 2011. Many had hoped that Ali's abdication would mark the start of a recovery, but if anything, the situation seemed to be getting worse. Even so, the ordinary people were determined to forget their woes whenever the opportunity presented itself.

It was the first day of Eid al-Adha, the Muslim festival marking the end of the annual Hajj to Mecca. The city streets were crowded with people, shopping and socialising in the relative cool of evening. Food was in abundance, with sweets on display everywhere. It was a time of fun and relaxation.

Families strolled along, the men one step ahead of their wives, and the children bringing up the rear. Many women sported the traditional *niqab* and *abaya*, covering them from head to toe – hardly ideal summer wear.

There were single young women to be seen too, ostensibly shopping with friends, but in reality more inclined to flirtation. At first glance, their movements suggested shyness; on closer inspection, their sweet smiles and erotic, inviting gestures were loaded with seduction. Single men, meanwhile, walked around loaded with hormones, hoping for the chance to grab a secret date with a girl. Or even – with a bit of luck – a brief sexual encounter.

The main entertainment, as always, was eating, with restaurants and cafes providing ample open-air seating. Large areas were occupied by families, the margins left to single men.

Somewhere amid the crowds, an old car shuddered to a halt; the driver was either reckless or extremely nervous. A teenage boy descended from the Chevrolet, urged on by the driver, who was anxiously reciting verses from the Quran.

The boy was, in fact, Abdul, and his enthusiasm was evident as he shouted '*Allahu Akbar!*' – God is Greater!

His eyes were sparkling with the determination to finish off Allah's enemies, those contaminated by Western civilisation. Months of brain-washing, combined with financial support for his family, had taken its toll on the already vulnerable young man. His thoughts and emotions were dominated by the dream of bettering himself in the afterlife. Finally, in a state of religious frenzy, he detonated the explosive vest, blowing himself to bits inside a restaurant.

There was a bright flash, an ear-splitting crack, and the already fragile walls of the restaurant were violently shaken. In the blink of an eye, the place became unrecognisable, a carnival of blood. There were bodies and body parts everywhere, littering the floor, gallons of blood mixed with food and ketchup. The victims were men, women and children, the elderly and the young. There was no discrimination as to class, wealth, age, gender or belief.

Abdul was evaporated, as if he had never existed. All those years of life and activity might never have happened.

There was a strange lull before the clamour began. Then the crowds gathered, and there was mass hysteria. The air was filled with the agonized cries of the injured and the shouts of rescuers.

Many victims were in agony on the floor, calling out, desperate for pain relief. Others were still in shock, checking to see what body parts were missing, numb to the pain that would hit them later with full force. Amid the chaos, passersby became good Samaritans, attending to casualties, trying to offer some consolation.

The passers-by were, in any case, much faster in responding than the emergency services, overstretched and underfunded as they were. Eventually, ambulance sirens could be heard, offering small consolation to people who had been happy diners just minutes before.

Abdul faded away into the ether, believing in his chances of a better life in the other world – better by far than the miserable existence he'd had on earth. He would never know how many lives he took with him, nor the permanent damage he had inflicted on the survivors; nothing but scars to remind them – until their dying days – of that horrific incident.

Chapter 9
Buenos Aires

In the Recoleta district of Buenos Aires – with its thriving art scene, fashionable boutiques and wine bars – stands the Four Seasons Hotel, a mix of modern and colonial architecture, boasting dozens of luxury suites. The hotel staff, like the guests, are normally cool and tranquil. However, on this particular morning, they were a swarm of activity.

Ramón, the hotel manager, had cut short his morning routine, including his coffee on the terrace, for today he had a special guest. The Royal Suite, reserved for the top businessmen and high-status dignitaries, was in need of preparation, and Ramón would supervise personally. Attention to detail was the rule.

There was also the question of security. Government intelligence agents had been to the hotel, checking the security measures. As always, a cloak of secrecy surrounded the hotel's incognito visitors, and the media were prohibited from approaching the premises. By mid-afternoon, with all preparations in place, it was just a matter of waiting.

Across the city – built in the image of Paris but with the added attraction of Latin spirit – it was a day like any other. The air was full of car fumes and the honking of horns. The streets were packed with people, busy as bees, yet somehow more relaxed than their North American cousins and European ancestors. In the Plaza de Mayo, locals and tourists strolled about, chatting and people-watching. In the cafes, they sipped coffee and munched on complementary mini-croissants, eyeing the passing strangers, including the swelling numbers of American tourists who made their presence known by their cheerfulness and acquisitive attitude.

With nightfall, the beautiful city was wrapped in darkness, tango music wafting from cafes and restaurants, the slender dancers spinning swiftly. Finally, through the darkness slid a black Mercedes, pulling up at the hotel entrance, where a special reception was waiting, headed by Ramón.

The concierge opened the car door and a pair of fine, slender legs emerged, complete with designer high-heels. It was Laura, wearing a rose-coloured dress with an abundance of flowers, the design in keeping with the Latin spirit.

'*Buenos días, señora,*' said Ramón, planting a kiss on the finely manicured hand.

Laura nodded politely and turned to help the gentleman next to her. It was Ali – or rather, what was left of him, as the British tabloids liked to joke. Before leaving London, he had been admitted to hospital with delirium tremens, and his stay had been extended due to a stroke that left him partially paralysed. The whole experience had left him emaciated and weak. His gait was slow, even with the help of a cane and Laura's loving hands.

Ramón was shocked to see how this once-lively man had ended up in such a miserable state. The hotel manager had done his homework, reading the latest developments in Ali's life – both the gossip and the hard facts. But he had never imagined things had gotten so bad.

He greeted Ali in a less-than-enthusiastic manner, and to his astonishment Ali answered in his heavily accented Spanish: '¿Cómo estás, Ramón?'

The hotel manager was surprised that Ali could recall his name; indeed, the shock left him momentarily speechless. They had, of course, met on several occasions over the years. Ramón recalled Ali serving as a diplomat in Buenos Aires before ascending to the throne, and he had visited the hotel more than once, always occupying one of the luxury suites.

Ramón's resume was more humble; he had spent most of his life in the hospitality industry, getting his start in Europe. He had returned to his native Argentina after the economic crisis of the military-junta; he was one of the victims of the Dirty War.

He had done various jobs, from working in bars to manning casinos, and even soliciting for high-society. He had always been in the shadow of others, never recognized for his work, always in a subservient role, one way or another. Finally, he had worked his way up to hotel manager, but he was still at the service of others, many of them less than gracious.

Now, with Ali's touch of kindness, he had been given a boost of vitality. He took hold of Laura's suitcase – despite the aches and pains in his knees – and placed it on the trolley, silently cursing the slow-moving porter.

A wheelchair was brought over for Ali, held firmly by another porter who was hoping for a generous tip. He had never before had the good luck to provide such a service for a wealthy prince, and he intended to make the most of it.

Ramón shoved the poor porter aside and took a firm grip of the wheelchair – not for the sake of the tip, but out of gratitude to a prince who made him feel he really existed. At the elevator, several hands held the doors open as Ali was wheeled inside.

In no time at all, they arrived at the suite and Laura took control of the wheelchair, thanking Ramón for his kindness. The door closed and – at long last – they were alone. Ali held Laura's hand and began to weep. She gently removed his sunglasses and began caressing his thick hair, which – on the recommendation of Jo, the Lebanese stylist – had been well oiled.

After the stroke, Ali and Laura had agreed to start afresh, far away in Argentina, a place he knew well from his days as a diplomat. Now they had arrived at their destination, and whatever feelings had been kept inside seemed determined to come out.

Ali tried to lift himself from the wheelchair, but his efforts were in vain. It wasn't so much paralysis that held him back – that had passed – but the weakened state of his muscles, which he had not used for months while he lay in hospital. Laura put her arms around him, and he felt his pent-up emotions boiling to the surface.

'It can't get any worse than this,' he said, his voice shaky and uncertain.

His pride prevented him from accepting help in standing, and so he chose to remain seated. Laura wheeled him into the bedroom, and as she set about the unpacking, Ali pondered recent events.

The British government had apologized for not allowing him to remain in the UK. The Home Office had been under pressure from the new government in Jawhar, which had threatened to cease cooperation in facilitating British contracts for a newly discovered – and very large – gas field.

Ali watched as Laura folded his silk pyjamas with her slender, nimble fingers.

'The British really were unhelpful,' he said, almost to himself.

Laura paused momentarily, then continued folding and smoothing the delicate material. They had been over all this before, of course, but there was no harm in doing so once more.

'They were basically asking you to go home,' she said, a shiver running unexpectedly down her spine. 'Not even the United States was kind to you,' she continued. 'You would think they'd allow you a visa to attend the Betty Ford clinic. But no, that was too much to ask, apparently.'

She sighed deeply and placed the pyjamas on a shelf. 'Of course, when one doors closes, another one opens,' she said, with a touch of brightness. 'The Argentinians have been so kind, and you've been lucky enough to secure some of your wealth here. I have some diamonds to sell and we will buy a farm at the outskirts of Buenos Aires. We will have children and live happily ever after.'

She stood looking at Ali, wondering how convincing her up-beat summary had been. She sank into the designer sofa, stretching out her slender, well-proportioned body, as if calling on him to rescue that gorgeous body from its demons. She arched her back and spread out more fully, luxuriating in the soft cushions, exhibiting her skills of seduction.

Even the prince's feeble frame, which had been exhausted by alcohol, smoking, stress and physical ailments, was not immune to the woman's charms. Grasping the arms of the wheelchair, he struggled to his feet, rejecting Laura's offer of help. He collapsed onto the sofa, squeezing her in his arms, fondling her firm breasts and frantically unbuttoning her Versace blouse.

She would have behaved differently with her clients; she had always been very assertive at work. But right now, she felt the need to be possessed by her lover, a feeling that had been denied all the while she was pursuing her career.

Ali felt himself being resurrected by Laura's angelic face. With no further need for words, he began kissing her neck, her breasts, armpits and stomach.

All of a sudden, just as Laura was nearing the height of arousal, he stopped. She found the abrupt termination of foreplay deeply annoying, and she cried out in anger and disappointment.

'What's the matter? Why have you stopped?'

Ali pushed himself free from her embrace and struggled to his feet. Standing on wobbly legs, one hand on the wheelchair, he began to cry like a baby.

'I can't manage it. I'm sorry, but I'm not a man anymore.'

The neurologist at the London hospital had warned him that the booze had likely caused some damage to his peripheral nerves. Among those areas affected were his genitals, with a significant decline in performance.

She sat forward and put to use one of her well-honed professional skills. Some of her older clients had experienced similar problems, and fellatio had often worked wonders. Before long, the combination of love and lust brought about a successful consummation, and Ali sank to his knees, his self-esteem somewhat restored.

Laura held his head between her breasts and whispered, 'I love you, darling, no matter what.'

At that moment, her words meant the world to him, and he felt himself smiling – a rare event these days. He heaved himself onto the sofa beside her, issuing a weary sigh of relief.

'Let's forget about the past and make a new start,' she said.

'Yes, let's do that,' he replied, unexpectedly flooded with optimism.

'I love the Hispanics,' she continued, lighting a cigarette. 'And their culture is very similar to your own.'

Ali did not disagree, but somehow he was suddenly too anxious to comment. The post-coital cigarette had reminded him of Laura's former life – a professional life spent in hotel rooms and luxury suites. That particular shadow continued to loom in their relationship, despite his best efforts to ignore it.

The distrust, meanwhile, was not all on one side. Laura was not sure she could ever be entirely trusting of a man who had fathered a dozen children by different wives, each of whom had been a princess or eminently respectable lady, and each of whom had benefitted greatly from his wealth. Not for the first time, she reflected that her main guarantee of his loyalty might be his own growing sense of inadequacy.

Ali had had enough of intimacy for the time being, and his thoughts drifted back to the Middle East. He picked up the hotel telephone and demanded access to the Arab television channels, requesting the latest Arabic newspapers delivered to his suite. He replaced the hotel phone and began flicking through his smartphone address book, searching for high-powered contacts in nations with which he had been on good terms in former times.

Laura knew what he was doing, and it made her angry. Within a matter of moments, he had switched from open-hearted intimacy to obsessing over the political situation, looking for more strings to pull, as if their 'new start' meant nothing.

She gripped his arm, and he looked up from the gold-plated mobile.

'I want you to swear to me,' she said, 'swear on whatever you believe, that you will care for me and never leave me.'

She was having trouble getting the words out; she cleared her throat and continued.

'Life has not been kind to me, Ali. It has taken from me everyone I once loved. My family is Catholic and conservative, very religious, as you know. They expected me to save myself for my future husband, but I rebelled against all that – even more so when I got to university in Paris. I got myself a boyfriend, François, and I gave him everything. Then he cheated on me with my best friend at university. You cannot imagine the humiliation. I really couldn't go through that again – or anything like it.'

She had Ali's full attention now. Her sad story and her sincerity tugged at his heart strings, and he folded her into his arms. Laura pushed him back very gently and looked deep into his eyes. 'Promise me you will never leave me,' she said.

Ali remained silent. He felt a strong desire to hear more, to learn more of the life struggle that had made Laura who she was.

'Meeting you has brought me back from the dead,' she continued. 'I have never felt so deeply for anyone, even François. When we broke up, I went a bit crazy. I decided to fix my financial problems by joining an escort agency. It worked financially, of course, but when François found out, he contacted my parents and sent them print-outs from the agency's website. I was on the website, listed among the options, and I was wearing almost nothing in the photographs. My poor mother was a miniature version of Mother Teresa. She couldn't cope – she almost died of a broken heart. My father didn't want anything to do with me. So I lost them too, in a way. And since then, I have hated men. I wanted to humiliate them, to deceive them, to fake orgasms in return for large sums of money, playing with their feelings. But you're different. You're someone I really love. You're all I have.'

The story was new to Ali, and he was shocked to hear it. He thought she had shared everything of importance, but this was new, and he was pained to learn of the hurt this sweet creature had endured. He was suddenly struck by Laura's ability to be simultaneously powerful and vulnerable; it was a mesmerizing combination.

Ali was desperate to offer some reassurance; this, after all, was a woman he loved deeply. However, something stopped him from doing so. His future looked unsettled at best, and he didn't want to make any promises he couldn't keep. He respected Laura more than that. He reached into his jacket and produced a Havana cigar. He sniffed it, hoping the familiar scent might lift the aura of sadness that hung about them both.

Then he spoke softly, so softly that he could hardly hear himself: 'We are all victims of ourselves.'

It was not, of course, what Laura was hoping to hear at the precise moment, but it was what he needed to say – and there was more.

'Sweetheart, I cannot give up my country,' he said at last. 'It is my past, present and future. I have my family and my children there, and they may be suffering the consequences of events. I have no ambitions to be head of state; I want to live a peaceful life with you. But I still have to know what is going on, and perhaps to take action. There are rumours that my father's properties have been confiscated, both at home and abroad. In addition, I am despised by all parties. My assets were frozen by various Western countries to appease the new rulers. I couldn't even stay in Europe. I'm in a very dark tunnel.'

He had started his speech with a certain firmness of voice, a clear-headed resolve. But that final sentence was uttered with a croak, and he found himself collapsing in tears.

Laura cradled his head in her arms, adopting the role of mother, a role to which she was becoming accustomed.

'We'll get through it together,' she said. 'I promise you.'

Chapter 10
In the Dragon's Den

In a small office in Beijing overlooking Tiananmen Square, three Chinese intelligence officials stood by the window chatting. The city was dusted in snow, but these men were nice and warm, thanks to the powerful central heating in this important government building.

They were speaking quietly, indifferent to the view from window, which took in several historic structures. At one end of the square was the mausoleum of Mao Tse-tung, while at the other was the Forbidden City, home to so many former emperors. In between, citizens of the People's Republic of China wandered around the vast, paved expanse, like so many ants, leaving tiny footprints in the snow.

The three officials spoke quietly so as not to be overheard by the fourth man in the room, a slender, nervous-looking official who sat alone at the far end of a highly polished table. From time to time, he would look in their direction and then look away again, examining his finger nails, wondering why he had been summoned.

The gentle chatter came to an abrupt halt as the door opened and a fat man in his mid-fifties entered the room. His dark suit was clearly expensive, and a pair of designer spectacles was perched precariously on his puffy moon-shaped face. Behind him was an assistant bearing a stack of cardboard files and bent almost double from years of kowtowing.

The fat man walked to his place at the head of the table, and the three officials scurried to their allotted seats, where they stood to attention, awaiting instructions. Out of respect and fear, they avoided eye contact with their boss; if he wanted them to look in his direction, he would let them know.

Mr Xi – known to his underlings as 'The Dragon' – squeezed his huge body into the elegant wooden chair, the arms of which creaked gently under the strain. He held out his hand, into which the assistant placed a beige file marked with the Chinese character for 'classified'.

Mr Xi was head of the Middle East section of the Political and Economic Intelligence Division at the Ministry of State Security. He came from a small village in southern China and his career journey thus far had been long and tough. He had fought hard to climb the ladder, making many sacrifices and crushing those who stood in his way.

Despite his powerful position, he was still haunted by his humble rural origins. He was well aware that, despite his best efforts, his village accent lingered. And it was perhaps for this reason that he tended to speak very loudly, as if seeking to stun others into submission.

At the far end of the table sat the solitary official, looking pale and worried. Ma Qixi hailed from Linxia Hui Autonomous Prefecture, an area of Gansu Province in the centre of China with a significant Muslim minority. In addition to his excellent Mandarin, he was fluent in Arabic, having studied the language at university and spent five years at the Chinese Embassy in Riyadh.

Ma had been handed an important role in the Chinese intelligence apparatus, an unusual honour for someone of his ethnic and religious background. He had worked hard to get to his position, and the Chinese system had rewarded his efforts. At this point in his career, he had some impressive achievements on his CV. His Muslim background and Arabic-language skills had made him popular with Arab officials, and he had been able to seal some very lucrative deals that benefitted China. Beijing was keen to take its share of the Middle East region's black gold, free from Western interference.

Mr Xi looked through the file, studiously ignoring everyone in the room. Ma wondered what exactly was in the file, and more importantly, why he had been summoned. Perhaps he had inadvertently made some error; perhaps a punishment was due. He felt his body begin to tremble, and he squeezed his hands hard to regain control.

The Dragon put the file down and began to speak, directing himself generally at Ma's end of the table. He launched loudly into some Chinese Communist Party rhetoric about the importance of the Chinese state and the brilliant leadership provided by the likes of Mao and his successors. Everyone nodded their agreement. After a couple of minutes, the speech came to an end, and Ma found himself pinned by Xi's hard, searching gaze. This was the last thing he wanted; he wondered what was coming next.

After a brief pause, the Dragon leaned over to his assistant and whispered something in his ear. The assistant stood and instructed everyone to leave the room. The three officials bowed gently and departed. Suffering simultaneously from mild confusion and great relief, Ma made to do the same, but he was stopped in his tracks by the assistant.

'Please take your seat again. Mr Xi wishes to speak with you alone.'

Ma sat down, his body now shaking like a leaf.

Mr Xi dismissed his assistant with a quick flick of the wrist and launched upon a well-polished speech about loyalty to the country and the ruling party. Two minutes later, the speech concluded, Xi sat in silence.

'I am a servant of the Party,' said Ma.

Xi looked him in the eye once more, apparently weighing up the pale figure before him.

'You know,' said Xi, 'Islamic fundamentalism presents an ongoing threat to the world, and China is no different. We are on the receiving end just as much as anyone else.'

The assistant re-entered the room briefly, remaining just long enough to place a porcelain teacup on the table. Mr Xi lifted the lid and took a sip of Korean Jinxing tea, which he drank more for its alleged aphrodisiac properties than its taste.

Ma cleared his throat and resumed the conversation: 'Sir, regardless of my faith, I am a loyal subject. I am a long-serving Party member, and my loyalty is to the Party and China, which I place before any religious considerations.'

Xi replaced the lid on his cup and looked at Ma. 'I want you to prove it to me,' he said.

'Please tell me what I can do. I will give my life for my country if necessary.'

Xi laughed out loud, a gesture that Ma found shocking. He had never thought of Mr Xi being capable of laughter, much less imagined what it might look like.

'No, don't worry. We need you alive,' said the boss.

Ma attempted a gentle laugh of his own, but his heart wasn't in it.

Mr Xi opened the file, read for a moment and then looked up again.

'I understand that you befriended Prince Ali when you served in the Chinese Embassy in Saudi Arabia. He was a frequent visitor to that country, and you left a great impression on him, apparently.'

Ma was startled; for the moment, he could not recall the prince of which Mr Xi spoke. Then it call came back, clear as day.

'Do you mean Prince Ali bin Kased? I understand that he was deposed.'

'Yes, he's the one,' said Xi, pushing his chair back to give his belly some more breathing room. 'As you know, Jawhar has one of the largest petroleum deposits in the Middle East. The Western powers, and particularly the Americans, are saving it for a rainy day. Once the traditional sources, such as Saudi Arabia, have run dry, they plan to tap this reserve. Assuming, of course, they have won the necessary concessions.'

'Yes, of course,' said Ma, glad to be on firm ground at last, discussing a topic on which he was well informed.

Then, to his great surprise, Mr Xi began to smile. It was not, apparently, a smile of cruelty, but one of kindness, the sort one might dish out to an old friend on their birthday. The smile was matched with a gentle change in tone of voice, from loud-hailer to the soft tones of a confidant.

'We want you to get in touch with Ali again,' said the Dragon.

'Why me, sir, of you don't mind my asking?'

Mr Xi smiled some more, and Ma wondered if he detected a hint of sarcasm on the man's lips, mixed in amongst all the camaraderie – perhaps even some of the resentment at Ma's fine pedigree and educational attainments.

'Well,' said Xi, 'you are fluent in Arabic and English, for a start. You know the Middle East region very well, and you have a solid background in petroleum-related issues. And, after all, you are a Muslim.'

This last word seemed to have been uttered with just a hint of disdain.

'But sir,' said Ma calmly, 'Prince Ali is not very religious, to my knowledge, and he leads a very Western lifestyle.'

'Well, they all do,' said Xi. 'But when it comes to trust, it's another story. Lifestyle to one side, religion still matters. And that's one advantage that you will take into the situation.'

Ma felt it wise not to argue any further.

'You will be summoned soon for a briefing on your mission,' said the boss. 'You may leave now.'

The smile was gone, and as Xi rang the bell for his assistant, Ma thought the man looked more like an old-time emperor. Seconds later, the assistant entered and escorted Ma from the room, handing him a small envelope on the way out.

Ma walked aimlessly across Tiananmen Square. Fresh snow was falling, blown about by the winter wind. He disliked the cold, but at least it lent the city a certain magical charm. The old buildings were charming enough, of course, but so much of Beijing was now covered in stark, modern buildings – soulless angular structures in imitation of the West.

Old and new now lived side by side, locked in a forced marriage for the benefit of the city's advancement. The process had been accelerated massively for the Olympic Games, of course; old neighbourhoods were flattened and new concrete or steel-and-glass structures thrown up. The government wanted everyone to see the gigantic economic miracle that was transforming China from a Third World country into the world's second economy – the manufacturing hub of Planet Earth.

Ma dodged a group of tourists from the provinces. They seemed to be enjoying themselves, posing for photographs amid the snowflakes. How nice it must be to live a simple life, unencumbered by great responsibilities – not to mention tests of loyalty.

He was puzzled by this new assignment. What exactly could they want? After all, the prince was out of power now. He had no power to dole out concessions. And why on earth should he trust Ma Qixi, a man he had known briefly and several years ago? Whatever did they have in mind?

He looked up and realised that his automatic pilot had turned him in the direction of Mao's tomb, the final resting place of the father of the Chinese communist state. As usual, several dozen visitors were lined up, waiting their turn to pay their respects to the embalmed corpse. Since his death 1976, Mao had been a constant figure in the minds of the people – a giant of history with near god-like status, despite his well-publicised errors.

Ma stood and watched the queue shuffling forward slowly. He recalled his first visit, as a child, to see the great leader. He had gone with his mother, who had explained afterwards that during the 1960s the middle classes had been targetted cruelly, dispossessed and branded class traitors. Ma's own family had been torn apart and sent to work in labour camps in various parts of the vast country. There had been millions of victims of Mao's Cultural Revolution, she had explained, and it was a good thing that Ma had not been alive to witness it.

Yes indeed, thought Ma. And yet, somehow the nation had survived, and even thrived under the guidance of subsequent leaders. And now his fellow Chinese citizens were enjoying the fruits of a miraculous economic boom, including the gradual process of modernisation and liberalisation.

He had benefitted from these changes, of course, and also from his career, nurtured by the state, despite his minority background. Now he was being entrusted with a task of great importance. He was being asked to prove his loyalty by accomplishing a most difficult mission: enlist Prince Ali to the service of his country.

He had no choice, of course, but to get the job done. No matter how difficult.

He walked on a little way and hailed a cab, glad to find shelter from the wind and snow. Sinking into the back seat, away from prying eyes, he reached into his jacket and pulled out the envelope. Inside was a letter from the Ministry of Foreign Affairs appointing him as cultural secretary at the Chinese embassy in Buenos Aires.

Chapter 11
The Sand Castle

The discussion was getting heated now. Voices were being raised, some in genuine anger. The men, many of them elderly, were all demanding solutions to the current crisis – and fast. Jawhar was facing mounting political turmoil, they said. With corruption still rife, the government had been unable to deliver on its many promises. The masses were demanding further changes, more of the democratic freedoms they saw being enjoyed abroad. With many investors putting their projects on hold, the economy was suffering. A pay rise for the public-sector workers had provided some breathing space, but not much.

Something must be done, but what?

The family meeting had been called in the throne room, in the presence of the new ruler, Prince Yousef, a cousin of Ali. At one end of the room was the throne, made of gold and ornamented with precious and semi-precious stones. Two dozen armchairs in Louis XIV style were arranged in two rows down the length of the room. They had been made with strict instructions to fit with the grandiose elegance of the palace, reflecting the wealth accumulated from oil sales.

This afternoon, however, the armchairs had been pushed back against the walls. They were not needed, for the elders preferred to sit on silky cushions on the floor, as they had done in their tents for so many generations. As a sign of respect to his elder male relatives, Prince Yousef did likewise, abandoning his throne for a cushion on the floor. Some of the younger royals, having been educated in Europe and the US, would have preferred the chairs, but they did as they were told.

The palace had been built by British contractors after independence. It had been decorated in the most luxurious style – imported marble, gold taps and priceless antiques from London. Since Ali's departure, however, there had been some notable changes in décor, with Yousef seeking to put his stamp on the place, declaring a new era in the nation's history.

Colour schemes and furniture had been revised, and the portrait of Ali was ripped from the wall. The grand wing containing Ali's harem and female relatives had been purged; now it was stuffed with Yousef's favoured females.

Today the relative calm of the palace had been shattered by the arrival of the elders, anxious to halt Jawhar's descent into chaos – and to protect themselves from personal ruin.

Low wooden tables had been laid before the cushions, and silver trays brought in bearing aromatic coffee. Dates had been provided, and Belgian biscuits. It was the perfect setting for a genteel discussion, but within minutes everyone was talking, competing to be heard.

The Arab Spring had brought irreversible changes, some said, but the change of leadership in this particular country had done little to calm the masses, who wanted more than just a face-lift; they wanted democracy, or at least wealth and freedoms. Three years had passed since the first protests, but heads were still rolling left, right and centre. Who could tell which of them might be next, scapegoated for the sake of the greater good?

Then, of course, there were the terrorist bombings. The *jihadist* forces seemed to be growing bolder by the minute. What would the terrorists do next? Would there be political assassinations – beheadings in the streets?

Meanwhile, those who had fled Jawhar had been unable to find refuge abroad – including Ali. Some of the elders said they had made plans to leave the country, sending millions to banks abroad and securing houses there. Others, meanwhile, were more inclined to stick it out, trying to contain the situation, one way or another.

A small minority were contemplating the reforms that Ali might have instituted, had he remained in power. They expressed nostalgia for the old days. Ali had been popular to some extent, especially with women and young, educated men. And he had been willing to make reforms – which might have helped.

The coup against him had backfired, they argued. By exposing the wealth of Ali and his court, it had exposed the nation's elite in general to greater scrutiny – and now nobody was safe. In such volatile circumstances, nobody could be sure how things might develop, least of all the national intelligence apparatus. Even the key Western intelligence agencies, MI6 and the CIA, seemed to be unsure.

Time was short, said one old man. There was nothing to be gained from arguing to and fro. What was needed was decisive action.

Yousef was a weak and fragile man, lacking the experience and training required for the job. As a spoiled young prince, he had failed his exams at Harvard University, hopping from one faculty to another in the hope of gaining some sort of qualification. Worse still, he was under the thumb of his mother, Princess Lolowa, a strong character, hardly conforming to her culture's model of the subservient female.

Unused to asserting himself, Yousef was dismayed by the pressure exerted by his elders, terrified at the possibility of jumping the wrong way. He had, of course, heard the reports from his intelligence officials. Some were warning of the imminent collapse of the new regime. They said they were swamped with security threats, including Islamic groups, which were competing to gain influence among the deprived, disadvantaged population. It was one thing to deal with peaceful protests, but quite another to fight an insurgency.

As the voices of disagreement, mourning, disappointment and complaint filled the room, poor Yousef became confused, agreeing and disagreeing at random with all factions. He cursed the day he had accepted the position of ruler.

Suddenly the quarreling stopped, all eyes turning to the far end of the room. A woman had entered – quite against palace rules – dressed head-toe in a black *abaya*, her *niqab* headdress leaving only a slit for the eyes.

'As-Salaamu Alaikum,' she said, her voice husky from smoking several *sheeshas* each day.

She walked to the centre of the room, standing among the group of men. In so doing, she further defied the rules of court that prohibit the mingling of the genders beyond strictly defined circumstances. Some of the young men stood as a sign of respect, but the elders remained on their cushions.

Aside from being Yousef's mother, Prince Lolowa was the wife of the founder of modern Jawhar. Her late husband had snatched power from the nation's other main tribe after the Second World War, arranging a coup d'état with the help of British intelligence. Lolowa had been involved in those events, and she had taken a keen interest in the birth of the independent nation. She felt her background implied a certain ongoing responsibility.

She was in her mid-seventies, but she looked strong enough to be in her forties. Her prominent body contours were visible through the long black robe, her presence accompanied by the expensive scent of Dehn Al-Oudh, the same perfume favoured by Ali's mother.

Within the family, Lolowa was respected and feared in equal measure. While some resented her interference in the business of men, it was agreed that she was a *femme sage*, a wily woman of great experience. Despite the huskiness, her voice was commanding, powerful as an opera singer's. She never had to give an order twice.

She sat in a chair next to the throne, the hall in deep silence as the assembled males awaited her first utterance. When it came, she spoke clearly and with confidence.

'My dear family,' she said, 'our country is having a hell of a time. If we are not careful, everything that we have built over many years could vanish, swept away in the course of an hour. I have personally sacrificed blood and sweat to get what we have now. The younger ones among you have palaces in Europe and America, money, lavish cars and beautiful women. But I got it the hard way, travelling in the desert on a camel, or in an oven-like jeep, if I was lucky. We fought, conspired, manipulated and even killed to get what we have today. I will not let you destroy it.'

The men sat open-mouthed as they listened to this old woman speaking – an old woman who could hardly read or write. The older men had always known her as a capable woman, and it seemed the passage of time had not changed a thing.

She adjusted her expensive *abaya* and began to speak in a stronger tone, as if rallying troops: 'We have to work together against our common enemies. There are many of them now, including Ali, who is our own flesh and blood.'

She turned to look at the prince, her eyes strict and threatening through the slit in her face-veil.

'Mother,' said Yousef, the fear quite apparent in his quavering voice, 'it was always my hope that we might avoid speaking so harshly of Ali.'

He eyes flared with anger, striking at his heart like a dagger.

She raised her voice: 'Shut up! While you sit here nattering, his supporters are conspiring to regain power. And what are you doing about it? Just sitting around and complaining when you should be taking action.'

She moved her bulky body, shifting position like a queen on a throne. As she did so, a faint and submissive voice was heard from among the men at her feet. It was a distant cousin, a man who once burned with desire for Lolowa. He knew that the years had only added more determination and experience to the matriarch.

'God prolong your life, lady,' he began. 'Ali is not making things easy for us. According to our intelligence services, he has some support among the common people, as well as friends in positions of influence.'

Lolowa slammed her hands down on the arms of the golden chair.

'Well, what do you expect?' she said. 'I am not a supporter of Ali, but even I must admit that he had his strengths. He went out of his way to make himself popular. He had charisma and charm. And he would never have tolerated the shitty sort of situation that we are facing now due to your ongoing mismanagement. If you want respect, you must earn it.'

She looked in disgust at the dignitaries seated on the floor. Drawing in a deep breath, she continued, her voice like thunder, 'We are now responsible for ruling this nation, and we must take that seriously. Nobody should be allowed to stand in our way, including Ali.'

With a slight movement of the head and a blink of the eyes, she indicated to the junior family members that they should leave. They politely got up and departed, aware that what followed would be confidential, confined to those with leadership roles.

Even those elders who had shouldered great responsibility in their time had not seen a situation so grave for decades. The last great upheaval was the withdrawal of British troops, followed by semi-independence and the confusion over who should lead the new nation. It had not been an easy time, with various powers keen to influence Jawhar's future.

When Lolowa spoke again, her voice was softer, hinting at a more calm and reasonable personality behind all the bluster.

'Listen to me, all of you. This is no time to make empty speeches. We are facing multiple threats, both from the people and – what's worse – from the international powers. We are not protected by our traditional allies, Britain and the United States. Now the Chinese have entered the game, asking for a piece of the cake – if not all of it. We are caught between a rock and a hard place. If we are to survive, we must fight our own battles.'

Lowola surveyed the elders for some reaction, but they were silent.

'Of course, certain people are seeking to have us eliminated, and my sources informed me today that a military coup could take place at any time. We have had our chances to assert ourselves and we have squandered them. We have had more than one opportunity to eliminate Ali, but these have come to nothing. He always seems to escape without a scratch. Any future attempts to resolve the problem must be decisive.'

She shifted again in her chair, choosing her words carefully.

'I don't think there is anyone here who wants to be a refugee, begging for a meal or a handout, bribing some head of state in order to gain protection. And nobody wants to be handed over to the next regime for execution or a life prison sentence.'

She suddenly rose to her feet, defying the layer of fat that had accumulated over the years. When she spoke again, it was with boldness and determination.

'We will destroy anyone who stands in our way. Death to the enemy!'

The men awoke from their trance, as if freed from a witch's spell. They rose to their feet and shouted: 'Death to the enemy!'

They repeated the rousing slogan several times, their voices bouncing off the luxurious palace walls.

Chapter 12
The Silk Route

Ma Qixi sipped his coffee and winced. He had never liked the stuff, despite drinking gallons of it during his years in the Gulf. He much preferred green tea. Sadly, the menu in this smart Buenos Aires café did not run to green tea. Anyway, he was determined to fit in with the local ways; this was, after all, an important mission.

The café was a popular spot next to the iconic Congress building – that imposing structure of white marble, with Roman columns and a huge dome. They had chosen the café for several reasons. For one thing, it was central, allowing Ali to slip out of the hotel and return within two hours. Added to which, the place was swarming with foreigners, making it the ideal spot for a Chinese spy and an Arabian prince to go largely unnoticed.

Finally, there was little chance of bumping into Laura. Ma had originally suggested a meeting at the hotel, but Ali had rejected the idea. The last thing he needed was Laura turning up and asking awkward questions.

Ali drank his coffee in rapid sips; he liked it hot and strong, and this place had it just right. He was enjoying both the new venue and the prospect of settling on a workable plan of action.

'Your Highness,' said Ma, 'everything is arranged and waiting for you. Our men in the palace and the army are waiting for your signal. Once you are in place, they will take the necessary action.'

Ma's inflammatory statements played well with Ali's ego, stoking his desire to regain the glory that had been lost.

They had already been over the basics of the proposal, and Ali was impressed. It was good to have such a powerful ally on his side, and the plan seemed pretty realistic. He was also content to keep up his end of the deal, providing China with a bigger share of oil and gas revenues.

Yes, this was a very welcome development, and it came not a moment too soon. Ali had been feeling vulnerable; he had failed to obtain asylum status in Argentina, despite having been stripped of his citizenship. For this reason alone, the prospect of a victorious return to his homeland was encouraging.

However, he hesitated to give his full consent just yet. For one thing, he knew that Laura was very much against him seeking to regain power. She had made her opposition very clear, finally refusing to discuss the subject. She said he should accept defeat in political terms and content himself with a new life based on the love between them. If they could just find a suitable place to settle, she argued, everything else would follow. However, since the rejection of Ali's asylum application, she had become increasingly distant. If she had any plans for their future together, she seemed to be keeping them to herself.

'I can't give my final consent just yet,' said Ali. 'We must find the right moment.'

'But the right moment is now,' insisted Ma. 'Everything is in place. We need to strike before the situation gets any worse. If you return now, you will be a hero. If you wait too long, the security situation may get out of control. Your firm hand is needed sooner rather than later.'

'I said we should wait,' said Ali. 'I have a number of other factors to consider. We will meet again to discuss this further.'

He looked at his watch and called for the bill.

'As you wish, Your Highness,' said Ma, draining his coffee cup with a frown.

* * *

Back at his hotel suite, Ali sat on the balcony surrounded flower pots, breathing the scent of tulips and carnations – his favourite flowers. He was thinking about Ma's proposal, turning it over and over, looking for a snag in the plan, a point of weakness that might result in failure.

His brain had been free from alcohol for some months now, and he had found his thinking clearer, his emotions more level. His general health was much improved too, thanks to the physiotherapist and the daily routine of exercise machines and dumbbells. It was almost as if he'd never suffered a stroke, never been confined to a hospital bed. This was good, because the course of action he was considering required a strong body and a calm, steady mind.

He went over the stages of the plan again. The coup would be swift and decisive, and with limited bloodshed. Arrests would be made, loyal military units deployed on the streets, the necessary announcements made through certain media channels. His disillusioned relatives, keen to regain their lost wealth and power, had already been brought on board. Jabber, Razak, Mahmoud and all the rest had been informed – and sworn to secrecy, of course.

Ali just needed to arrive at the critical moment, and everything would slot into place. He must first travel to another Latin country, from which he would fly to a neighbouring Arab state. From there, he would be smuggled across the desert into Jawhar.

His thoughts turned to David Lean's film Lawrence of Arabia: the camels crossing the desert, plodding on for days in the blistering heat.

But this was no film. It was reality.

What were the consequences of defeat? He would suffer horribly in prison, perhaps being executed for treason, or else tortured to death. But his family would also suffer. There would be another purge, and nobody would be spared this time.

Even if he succeeded, there might be a terrible price to pay in personal terms. How would his relationship with Laura endure such a deception? Would she trust him again? And if so, how would they continue their intimate relations while he struggled to assert his authority as ruler?

She had stood by him thick and thin, supporting him on the tortuous journey through addiction to recovery, comforting him in his humiliation, providing company in exile. She had even helped with his financial needs, selling her jewelry and leaning on heads of state to release some of his confiscated funds. Due to her persuasive powers, a number of powerful men had provided loans at reasonable rates.

And now he was repaying her by plotting behind her back. It was a betrayal of sorts, and he hated himself for it.

He looked down from the balcony at the hotel guests around the swimming pool. They lay in the sun, snacks and cocktails arranged on little tables. Children splashed in the pool, blissfully unaware of the ways of the world. How wonderful, he thought, to be carefree, to be free from all obligation and responsibility.

Of course, thought Ali, there was no certainty that Laura was not engaged in some plotting of her own. She had been ominously quiet these past few weeks; quiet and distant, and mostly absent from the hotel. She had started taking Spanish classes, part of her plan to gain citizenship in some Latin American nation. But he couldn't help wondering what she did in between lessons, and in the evenings before her late return each night.

After his asylum application had been rejected, she had visited the US Embassy to renew her expired passport. It was a routine procedure, just a trip to the consular section. But the embassy had rolled out the red carpet for Laura, the ambassador insisting on a personal meeting over lunch.

Details of their discussion had been relayed to Washington, and soon she and Ali received invitations to an embassy party. Ali was still angry with Washington for rejecting his visa application, and his first instinct was to throw the invitation in the ambassador's face. However, Laura brought him round, insisting that there was no harm in nurturing friendships at the embassy. After all, one never knew where such things might lead.

Ali tagged along, shaking hands with the ambassador and engaging in empty chit-chat for an hour. He met the ambassador's wife too, and a number of foreign dignitaries, although thankfully nobody from the Arab world. Even so, some of them seemed embarrassed about meeting a recently deposed leader – an alcoholic too, so rumour had it.

It didn't help that waiters kept offering him alcohol – an offer he was forced to refuse for the sake of his health.

A week later, another invitation was sent out, and Laura said they should accept. But this time Ali put his foot down. Laura could go if she wanted, but he would stay home. Why subject himself to such humiliation for the sake of sucking up to the Americans? Most likely, he said, they just wanted to keep him close in order to prevent him making alliances elsewhere.

Since then, Laura had been back to the embassy several times. She had even stopped mentioning the fact, returning in the early hours and slipping quietly into bed beside Ali. He would pretend to be sleeping, but really he was wide awake, thoughts racing, teeth clenched.

Who was betraying who? If she was being disloyal – as he often suspected – what right had she to demand loyalty of him? Why shouldn't he act alone, in secret, for the sake of his future, his country?

He picked up the phone and ordered some lunch. He wanted to order a bottle of whisky, and for a brief moment, he considered doing so – but he knew it would only lead to ruin. Now more than ever, he must remain clear-headed.

Ma was certainly right about the gravity of the situation and the need for swift action. According to local intelligence reports – copies of which Ali still received through his embassy contacts – Jawhar was heading down a slippery slope. Religious fundamentalist groups were gaining in size and power, recruiting new followers each day. Small terror cells were growing into efficient bands of guerrilla fighters, acquiring weapons from somewhere. Soon the security forces would be overwhelmed; there was no telling what might follow.

Foreign intelligence agencies had reached similar conclusions. There had been several attacks on foreigners in the county, with many people injured and killed. Now foreign diplomats, particularly the Westerners, were barricaded inside their embassies and high-walled compounds – like hostages, fearing the next attack.

Western governments were banging the drums of war, keen to protect both their subjects and their interests. Keen also to win a larger slice of the oil revenue. The US Navy had been deployed along the shores of the tiny Arab state, joined by a symbolic naval presence from the British, keen to give some moral support to their Anglo-Saxon cousins.

The Chinese, meanwhile, were keeping a low profile in Jawhar. Ma said the embassy's busy commercial department had made way for a team responsible for planning the change of regime. They had put all the pieces in place, updating Ma through the embassy in Buenos Aires. Now they just needed the green light and a firm date.

Ali knew he was nearing a decision. If Laura wanted to stop him, then she should open a conversation, come clean about her late nights, convince him that he hadn't already been betrayed. In the absence of such reassurances, perhaps he had every right to act alone.

* * *

The following Tuesday, Ali and Ma met again, this time in a restaurant off the Plaza de Mayo. They had chosen a table on a balcony, which offered a fine view of this historic quarter – and a little privacy.

Over beef steaks, Ali announced that he had reached a decision: the coup would go ahead, and soon. He was ready to become the saviour of his nation. Lolowa and her puppets were incompetent and declining in popularity. The people were longing for Ali to return, ushering in a period of security and popularity. There was no point in delaying further.

'This is great news, Your Highness,' said Ma. 'Once the travel arrangements are finalized, everything will go smoothly. You can trust that every detail has been considered at our end.'

'This is very reassuring,' said Ali, pouring himself another glass of water.

'Of course,' continued Ma, 'success depends upon secrecy. You must tell nobody about this. You should trust only me.'

Ali sipped his water and looked Ma in the eye.

'What about Laura?'

'I think it best to keep her out of it, Your Highness, considering the concerns you have expressed.'

'I'm not planning to tell her, of course, but she may find out for herself. Laura is a very clever woman, and we spend some time together every day, if only at breakfast. She has a way of getting the truth out of me.'

For the first time in many years, Ma felt a sense of importance, as if he were a big fish, not some tiny sprat in the great ocean of Chinese bureaucracy. He had had enough of being a nameless entity shuffled from place to place in line with other peoples' plans.

Using his best classical Arabic, he leaned forward and spoke quietly: 'Your Highness, it is an easy matter. There is no need for you to be concerned. We will sort her out.'

Ali was enraged, his face flushing red, eyes wide. He stood up, his six-foot frame towering over Ma. He grabbed the Chinaman by the collar.

'Don't you ever DARE to hurt Laura!' he yelled.

'Forgive me, Your Highness,' pleaded Ma, alarmed at this sudden turn of events. 'No one would dare to touch her. She will be fine.'

Ali returned to his seat, conscious that his outburst had caught the waiter's attention. He drained his glass and poured more water.

'I will hold you to that, Mr Ma,' he said, still fuming.

'Of course, Your Highness,' said the spy. 'You can rely on me absolutely.'

Ma pulled out his wallet and counted out some notes, placing them on the table. He then rose unsteadily to his feet and bowed again.

'Until next week then,' he said.

Ali cut a slice of steak and stuffed it into his mouth.

As he left the restaurant, Ma felt like a Chinese bureaucrat departing the Forbidden City after a difficult audience with the emperor. Shaking like a leaf, he walked to the Plaza and hailed a cab.

'Waiter!' shouted Ali. 'Bring me some brandy!'

Chapter 13
Bad News

Ali woke to the sound of Laura's footsteps as she moved hastily around the hotel suite. She already had her shoes on, the heels clacking on the marble floor. Clearly, she was in a rush, but he had no idea why.

His head was still thick from the night before; it had not been a restful night. Laura had been out at a party of some kind, and Ali had taken the opportunity to fall off the wagon. He had settled down on the sofa with a bottle of whisky, flicking through the TV channels and deciding finally on some shallow action movie; anything to distract him from his anxieties.

Laura had returned after midnight to find him drunk and in tears, the bottle empty on the coffee table. She had put him to bed, scolding him for going back on his promise to steer clear of the booze. He had risen to the bait and they had argued furiously.

What right had she to tell him what to do with his life? Why on earth shouldn't he drink if he wanted to? Hadn't his life been hard enough?

Eventually, he had dissolved in tears again, full of remorse and self-loathing. Before going to sleep, he had promised to see a psychiatrist. There were plenty in Buenos Aires, which had one of the highest per-capita concentrations of shrinks on the planet. He might even find one that spoke Arabic; there were plenty about, apparently.

Now he sat on the edge of the bed and squinted into the bright light of morning. He asked Laura what she was in such a panic about. She was standing by the wardrobe, yanking out dresses and tossing them into a suitcase, crying all the while.

'It's my father,' she said. 'He's had an accident and was admitted to hospital.'

She cleared her throat and added: 'They called me to say I should go and see him because it may be my last chance. That's what the doctor at the hospital told me anyway.'

Ali got up and walked over to her, holding her tight, hoping that no harm would come to his darling Laura or her family. He kissed her face, which was wet with tears.

'Darling,' he said, 'you must do what you think is best for you. I will be fine.'

She wiped her tears with her bare hands and whispered, 'But what about you? I want to support you.'

He stroked her thick blond hair; his touch had a calming effect on her frayed nerves.

'You've already done so much for me. Now I will be strong for you, just as you were for me. You are my rock.'

His eyes were filled with tears; he knew he wasn't telling the whole truth.

The hotel was in the process of booking Laura's air tickets. They had been more than helpful, rushing to ensure she made it home as soon as possible. 'Home' these days meant Florida; her parents had finally abandoned New York with its freezing winter weather.

Laura telephoned Florida, but her mother refused to speak with her. She blamed her daughter for the family's various misfortunes. However, Laura's younger brother was reasonable enough to explain the drama, how her father was hit by a car while crossing the road near their suburban house. He had apparently been the victim of a hit-and-run accident; it was just a freak event.

Laura was torn between her love for her family and her concerns that Ali might return to his old ways. After all, the previous night had been bad. It was months since she'd seen him in the role of raging drunk. This seemed the very worst moment to be ducking out.

She held his hand and said softly: 'Ali, promise me in the name of your late mother that you will not touch alcohol while I'm gone – and please look after yourself.'

Ali was shocked; his mother was the most sacred and pure thing in his life. He felt uncomfortable associating his mishaps with his divine mother. At the same time, he felt relieved that Laura would be out of the way. After all, he had other plans.

'Darling, I promise that alcohol will not come between us. We will marry and have children and they will live in their father's country.'

Laura gave a look of revulsion, yanking herself free from Ali's gentle grip.

'What do you mean? You're not going to do anything stupid in my absence, are you?'

Ali was startled both by her reaction and his apparent inability to keep a secret.

'No, darling,' he said softly. 'I'm just hoping the situation in the Middle East will settle down one day and we can travel freely.'

The telephone rang and Laura rushed over to it. Ali let out a sigh of relief.

The receptionist said the flights were booked. Laura should be ready to travel in two hours. A car would take her to the airport. She thanked the receptionist and returned to her packing. She had no time to drag a promise from Ali.

Three maids arrived at the suite and began to help with the packing. They fluttered around Laura like butterflies around a flower. The moment of departure came, and the bell boy wheeled the luggage downstairs. Ali and Laura lingered in the suite, savoring a farewell kiss. The Latino maids stood in the corridor listening to the romantic sentiments and heartfelt emotions. They were all dreaming of having their own Prince Charming one day – a true *cariño* like Prince Ali.

Chapter 14
Stars in the Desert

The Bedouin caravan snaked through the rocky desert landscape. Above, the sky was clear, but a keen wind was blowing from somewhere, transporting grit and sand mile after mile. The wind whistled around the dry wadis and rocky outcrops like a ney – that traditional wooden flute so suited to sad melodies.

But this was no traditional caravan, no snaking line of camels. These were hardy four-by-four vehicles, the preferred mode of transport of the modern Bedouin, and they threw up clouds of dust as they motored steadily onward.

Inside were a dozen tall, slim men – toned and sun-baked, thoroughly at home in this unforgiving landscape. They each wore a long white *deshdasha*, combined with a black *abaya* made from goat wool. It was the job of the senior ladies in the tribe to weave these *abayas* – women of high social status, respected for their wisdom.

These men had no interest in taking up a comfortable existence in air-conditioned houses. They preferred their hard desert life, enduring the heat of the sun during daytime, the shivering cold of nighttime. And who could blame them? After all, there is nothing so spectacular as the starry skies of the desert. In Mediaeval times, Arab astronomers gave names to the constellations and used them as navigation aids on their long desert journeys. The modern Bedouin has the advantage of GPS technology, but the natural environment is no less demanding, the line between life and death still fine. Such tough lives produce people endowed with endurance, people with self-reliance at their core.

The caravan was on high alert as it snaked through the rocky terrain. The anxiety felt by the men stood in contrast to their normally relaxed, laissez-faire attitude. The reason was their high-value cargo, perhaps the most precious human cargo they had ever escorted.

The second car of the convoy was a dust-coloured Honda, driven by a quiet middle-aged man with grey stubble and dark sunglasses. Beside him in the front passenger seat was a young-looking middle-aged man with a slim, toned figure. This younger man likewise sported dark glasses, but his were considerably more expensive, for this was Faysal, the son of the tribe's chief. Faysal had taken on many more responsibilities since his father's health began to fail, and he was now the *de facto* head of the tribe. Many considered him young for the role, and he often wondered if this was true.

In the back seat of the Honda were Ali and Ma, rocking with the movement of the vehicle, watching in silence as mile after mile of desert passed by the windows. Ali was glad to be back in his homeland, and even more glad to be deep in the desert, a landscape that was so central to his identity and that of his people. Yes, it was good to be back; only now could he see how deeply he'd missed his country.

His thoughts skipped to the practicalities of his covert mission, in particular the amount of money to which he had access and how long it would last. A project such as this was horribly expensive; building alliances and greasing palms was never cheap. And then there were his personal expenses, which were piling up by the day. He had scraped together everything he could, but there was little room for error.

Next to Ali sat a small man with oriental features. It was Ma, the former resident of Beijing who had made such a deep impression on Faysal's tribe in recent weeks. They were over the moon that a Chinese official – an exotic person in their eyes – had studied their own dialect, thereby recognizing them as people of importance.

As Ma gazed at the passing shrubs and rocks, he pondered the preparations that had been made in case their plot was discovered or their convoy ambushed by security forces. In his bag were documents suggesting his identity as an Islamic terrorist from China – a move designed to insulate the Chinese government from suspicion. He sat with his hands in his jacket pockets, a fast-acting cyanide capsule held lightly in his slender fingers. He rolled the capsule gently between thumb and finger, just to be sure of its presence. This was one element of the plan of which Ali had not been informed.

The three men sat in silence as they motored onward. They had already been over the basics of the plan; there was no point in further discussion before they arrived at their destination. The elders of the tribe were waiting patiently, and they would no doubt have a few questions of their own when the time came.

Half an hour later, the convoy arrived at its destination – a small valley between low hills, blessed by a spring, a well and some trees providing shade. In the centre sat a traditional goat-wool tent, held aloft by poles and tied down with dozens of ropes, staked into the hard ground. The jeeps approached cautiously, keeping their distance until two elders emerged from the tent, flanked by armed guards.

Faysal stepped from the Honda and opened the door for Ali and Ma, who left the vehicle's air-conditioned interior and crossed the stretch of warm earth. The two senior elders greeted Ali with a mixture of warmth and deference, exchanging kisses on the cheeks.

Entering the tent, Ali saw a dozen men, elderly and middle-aged, standing in a circle, dressed in *deshdashas*, cushions at their feet. The floor was covered in brightly coloured rugs, and the air – much cooler than outside – was fragranced with incense. Younger men with weapons were arranged around the perimeter.

Ali was shown to a cushion at the far end of the tent, and everybody sat down. After introductions, chilled water was served, followed by fresh-ground, aromatic coffee, cooked over a bare flame and served with great ceremony.

Eventually, Faysal began to address the assembly. He spoke with heroic bravado, first reciting verses from the Quran as proof of his sincerity and commitment. The elders listened in silence, all eyes on their young leader.

Ali had known this tribe for many years and had enjoyed several long discussions with Faysal's father. However, the crafty old man was now suffering from Alzheimer's disease, and he sat far away in his own living-room, unaware of unfolding events. Ali had not really paid attention to Faysal as a youth, and now that he was seeing the man up close, he was not particularly impressed.

The son seemed to possess none of the skills required by the convoluted political environment of this volatile corner of the world. It was anyone's guess how he would handle a covert operation such as that being proposed.

Ali decided there was little point in pondering worst-case scenarios. After all, he thought, beggars can't be choosers. So long as the instructions were passed down the chain of command clearly, everyone should know their job and act accordingly.

Once Faysal had finished with his preamble, he handed over to Ma, who began to explain the plan of action, while the elders listened intently.

Ma knew whole thing by heart: names, dates, places, entrances, exits, palaces and personalities. The army was on Ali's side, with some of the senior officers drawn from Ali's own tribe, while others were his cousins. The soldiers themselves were mainly foreign nationals and could be classified as mercenaries. Their allegiance went to the highest bidder, and Prince Ali had sufficient funds to stuff their pockets with gold. Once the plan was put into action, all the Bedouin tribes would be siding with Ali, explained Ma, and they would confirm their support through a *bay'ah* – the traditional Islamic pledge of allegiance. The particular role of Faysal's tribe was laid out in some detail, with their objectives well defined.

Thus far, every one of the elders seemed impressed with the plan, confident that they were wise to be siding with Ali. However, Ma's next comment sent a ripple of concern through the tent.

'And you can rest assured that we already have a plan for taking care of Princess Lolowa, the mother of Prince Yousef. I cannot tell you the details of our plan, but I can assure you that she will not cause any further problems for Prince Ali.'

The response was pretty much as expected: the elders' eyes widened, their eyebrows raised, and they turned to their neighbours, expressing both excitement and concern. Soon the room was alive with discussion; it was as if Ma had thrown gasoline onto a bonfire. To these men, many with memories of past conflicts, the woman's name inspired fear. She was like some beast from a horror film, famous for its power and cruelty, and any attempt to take her on was either heroic or foolhardy.

Faysal had never met Lolowa, but her name hit him like a slap in the face, for he was well aware of the woman's mythical status. He found himself trembling at the thought of opposing her in open rebellion.

In a voice loaded with fear and insecurity, he said to Ma: 'Do you intend to target Princess Lolowa directly? She is a vile creature, very dangerous.'

'Yes, the princess is a formidable woman,' continued Ma, 'and she seems determined to oppose Prince Ali's return. Our intelligence sources inform us that she is already taking steps in that direction. Indeed, she may have been behind the attack in France. This is to be expected, of course; she has a reputation for asserting her wishes. But we are confident that we can eliminate Princess Lolowa before she can take decisive action. You need not worry about the details. We have everything in hand.'

The Chinese spy looked around the room to gauge the response, which was not entirely encouraging. The men had descended again into private discussions with their neighbours, and he could tell that fear was the dominant sentiment in the room.

'She must be taken out decisively, or not at all,' said Faysal, speaking for everyone in the room.

'This is why we have devised a concrete plan of action,' said Ma, raising the voice above the babble. 'We need to shut her up forever. And we will.'

If there had been any doubt about what was being asked of the elders, this had now been eliminated. They were being called upon to back a coup that would involve the killing of Princess Lolowa – a woman would surely take a terrible revenge if the coup failed.

'But Lolowa is totally ruthless,' said one of the elders, speaking for his peers, and apparently not convinced by Ma's reassurances thus far.

Ma responded firmly, hoping that he would not have to repeat himself again: 'Don't worry. We will sort her out.'

Faysal was looking pale now, sitting quietly as he absorbed the seriousness of the mission. He watched the elders for a while as they continued to chatter, finally clapping his hands and calling them to order.

'Be quiet please, and listen,' he said. 'Have some faith that Mr Ma knows what he is doing. Prince Ali would not have invested himself in this project if he were not entirely confident of its outcome. For my part, I have no doubt that Lolowa will be dealt with swiftly and decisively, and I ask you to also have faith. We are all committed to supporting the return of Prince Ali, and if this is what it takes, then we shall make the necessary efforts. I have full confidence in the plan as it has been outlined. I am entirely at Prince Ali's service.'

The elders listened patiently and respectfully, but Faysal's words could not erase the signs of worry on the faces. These men, normally considered alpha males, seemed to be suffering a rare moment of self-doubt.

Ali had been watching in regal silence, taking in every detail of the interactions, seeking to gauge the mood – and the likelihood of this tribe performing their duties as expected. So far, he was not particularly impressed with the courage or resolve of the elders in the face of Lolowa. However, there didn't seem to be much in the way of alternatives; the plan had been worked out already in great detail, and there was no backing out now.

Some of elders were looking in his direction, perhaps expecting him to provide a rousing speech, or at least a word of reassurance. But he felt this would be superfluous; it was for Ma to explain the project and for Faysal to provide leadership to his tribe. A prince should not be expected to get his hands dirty with too many details; after all, a certain distance was required if one was to maintain respect.

Finally, Ali stood up, indicating that the meeting was at an end. The assembly of men likewise got to their feet, bowing their heads slightly in the royal presence. He extended his hands, inviting the elders to approach and shake hands with him individually before his departure. They did so gladly, smiling warmly and expressing their loyalty with traditional utterances.

'*Ala Barakat Allah*,' they said, as he walked from the tent – With God's blessings.

Chapter 15
Hit and Run

Laura sat in the hospital waiting room, staring at the television on the wall as it flickered silently, pumping out images of Middle East turmoil. The news channels were relentless in their coverage of the unfolding disasters in the region: the wars, the terror, the failing states and embattled rulers.

Her father had been taken to the Mayo Clinic in Jacksonville, Florida, and Laura had been at his side for the past 48 hours, sitting in intensive care and clutching his hand as the machines beeped. Now she needed a moment to herself, just to sit alone with a coffee and sort through the wreckage.

Her mother was distraught, unable to comprehend the chain of events, much less provide Laura with any sensible explanation for his injury. All she knew was that her husband had been horribly injured and now lay in a coma. Laura had spoken with both the police and the clinic doctors, but she couldn't make the pieces fit.

The police reports said he was the victim of a possible hit-and-run incident. However, there was some discrepancy between the witness statements. An anonymous caller had dialled 911 from a pay-phone, stating that he'd just seen a hit-and-run accident, but this anonymous witness had fled the scene and was never identified. Another witness had given a statement at the police station, but he only said that he'd seen the victim walking on the pavement one minute and lying in a pool of blood the next. The witness had not seen the incident itself because he was distracted by a phone call from a friend. He did say that he heard the screech of tyres at some point, but he couldn't say more than that.

Meanwhile, the doctors said their patient had suffered a head trauma resulting in serious brain damage. The injury was consistent with an attack with a blunt object, although a vehicle collision was also possible. However, there were no broken bones, abdominal injuries or lacerations – none of the injuries often associated with a hit-and-run. When Laura pressed them on the subject, the doctors were non-committal.

There was something fishy about her father's situation and Laura was determined to find out what it was. She had enough life experience to know the value of being sensitive to danger. In the course of her career, she had dealt with numerous difficult personalities – including a few psychopaths and sadists – and her nose for danger was now well developed.

She returned to the intensive-care unit and sat looking at her father, with drips in his arms and tubes emerging from his nose and mouth. Suddenly an image from her childhood flashed into her mind; she was playing with her father, being cuddled and pampered. How happy she'd been back then, safe in his arms, safe in the heart of a loving family.

And then it had all changed. She had been sexually abused by a family friend, an event that had left a black mark on her childhood memories. Nobody wanted to believe her, insisting that she had been mistaken. After a while, she had started wondering if she had invented the whole thing. How sad it was that such an event should ruin the otherwise loving connection she had had with her family, particularly her dear father.

As she watched him lying there in the hospital bed, his chest rising and falling slowly, his head swathed in bandages, Laura resolved to find those responsible for this crime. Her brain sprang into action, searching for links between events in her recent personal life and her father's unfortunate accident – if indeed it was an accident. She reached into her huge leather handbag and dug out her smartphone.

She opened the address function and began searching for the number of Jimmy Mitchell, the cultural attaché at the United States embassy in Buenos Aires. She had no doubt that he was really a CIA officer. He had approached her in Buenos Aires, asking her to keep an eye on the prince, particularly his links to any undesirable foreign contacts that might harm US interests in the Middle East.

At first, Laura had been torn between the love of her life and a sense of patriotic duty. However, she eventually came to feel that cooperation with her government was a win-win situation. After all, her relationship with Ali was bound to end the moment he regained his position as head of state, and if she could help to foil any such plans, then so much the better. So she agreed to be the eyes and ears of her nation, wishing above all else for a happy ending of the romantic variety.

She had intercepted Ali's phone calls and recorded the Arabic-language conversations, passing everything to her embassy contact. She had even probed Ali on his future plans, all the while trying to draw him into a normal, quiet life on a ranch in Argentina, surrounded by gauchos and tango music. For a while things had seemed to be hopeful, but she was never sure that she had the full picture. She suspected that something was afoot, that he was plotting a coup. She had informed her contact of her hunch, but she had no proof. Ali had withdrawn large sums of money from his Panama bank account, but Laura didn't know where it was being spent.

She continued flicking through the contacts on her smartphone, trying to remember how she had saved Jimmy's number. She'd used some clever nickname as a means of disguise, but right now her mind was a blank. She stopped at Jimmy Jordan, thinking this might be the one, and pressed the call button. The voice that answered was soft, masculine and strangely familiar.

'Hi Laura. Good to hear from you,' he said.

'Hello,' she whispered.

'I tried to call you when I was in Paris,' continued the man. 'I thought perhaps we could meet up.'

Laura was confused. Was this her intelligence contact? Presumably not, because this man was speaking with an upper-class English accent. Was this perhaps another Jimmy from her former life as a high-class escort? Her head began to spin. She looked more closely at the number and saw the UK dialing code.

Then it all came back to her. Yes, Jimmy Jordan was a very special client from London, a man who had treated her like a princess. He was young, good looking and something important in banking. He was also in the habit of making political donations and had won some influence in the British political scene.

He had treated her like a loving husband but she had never been sure of the truth depth of his feelings, shielded as they were by gentlemanly English manners. She often climaxed while making love with him, which was a rare occurrence for her during working hours. For a moment, she felt the urge to drop everything and rush into his arms. Would it really be so bad to go back to her old ways? And didn't she have feelings for Jimmy Jordan anyway? What if those feelings were truly reciprocated? Perhaps she could just forget her current troubles and start again from scratch?

Suddenly aware of the silence on the line, Laura snapped back into the present moment and her responsibilities as a daughter.

'Jimmy, my darling, I'm so sorry! I dialled your number by mistake. How are doing?'

She heard a happy sigh at the other end.

'I'm fine,' he said. 'I want to see you very soon. Where are you? The madam told me that you had left the company, and then I read somewhere that you've moved to Argentina. Is that true?'

Laura found her patience running out. She had a lot to do and no time for chatting. Even so, she did not want to upset a gentleman who had been extremely kind to her – not to mention being generous with the cash.

'I'm in the States dealing with a family emergency,' Laura said. 'I'm sorry, Jimmy, but I have to go. I'll call you soon.'

She heard the disappointment in his voice.

'Oh, I'm sorry to hear that,' he said. 'Please do get in touch if you decide to come to London. I will pay all your expenses if you decide to visit.'

'That's very kind of you. Goodbye, Jimmy.'

And she hung up.

As she sat looking at the phone, it occurred to her that an all-expenses-paid trip to London might not be a bad idea. Jimmy Jordan was wealthy, and she could certainly do with the cash. Moments later, she was shocked at herself, dismayed that she could even contemplate such a course of action. Had she really drifted so far from her beloved Ali that she would contemplate returning to her old ways? She decided that she must be over-tired; exhaustion was known to play tricks on the brain.

She returned to the address book and continued scrolling back and forth. Then she spotted it: 'Jimmy culture'. Yes, was right. She pressed the button and the call was answered by a loud American voice. It was the familiar Texan voice of her embassy contact.

'Well hello, my dear Laura! How are you? Where are you?'

'I'm in the States,' she said, hesitantly.

'Welcome home! I'm here too. I have some work to attend to in D.C. Maybe we could catch up?'

Laura's strong fifth sense sniffed a plot. Why was he here in the States now? Why had he left Argentina at the same time as her? Had he known about her father's accident in advance? Or was that just paranoia? US cultural attachés no doubt did a lot of travelling, and D.C. was probably high on the list.

She took a breath and said, 'I'm not okay, I'm afraid. My father is seriously ill in hospital, at the Mayo Clinic in Jacksonville, Florida. He was struck by a car. It was a hit-and-run accident – or maybe it wasn't an accident.'

'What do you mean?" he asked.

'Listen, I won't to go into details over the phone, but I've been working with you for a while now, risking my neck to serve my country. As a thank-you gesture, would you please tell your people to investigate this attack on my dad? Then – and only then – I will discuss Ali's recent movements with you.'

Not waiting for a reply, she hung up.

She thought the gesture implied power, as if she had the upper hand – but she knew this was probably not true. Jimmy was hardly one to be pushed around. And anyway, she was clueless about Ali's movements; her calls to various phone numbers around the world had gone unanswered. She could only speculate on his whereabouts now. Perhaps he'd returned to Europe or the Middle East? Question after question paraded through her mind, but no answers were forthcoming. Her gut instinct was that something sinister was about to happen to Ali – or had already happened.

Exhausted, she returned to her hotel – not far from the hospital – and took a nap on the bed. She hadn't had a good night's sleep for so long, and she was dead on her feet. She was woken by the insistent ring of her smartphone.

'Hello,' she croaked.

'Laura darling, your father has passed away.'

It was her mother, speaking from the hospital, her voice somehow vague and indistinct.

Laura was struck dumb, unable to respond or acknowledge this terrible news.

'Can you hear me, Laura? Your father's passed away.'

The mother's tone of voice was soft and sympathetic, by Laura wondered whether she detected a slight tone of resentment. After all, Laura had always been closer to her father than to her mother.

'Laura, can you hear me?'

She was unable to respond, caught up in a chain of memories: the father hugging his daughter, sharing his love – something the mother had always had difficulty with; the sexual abuse of a child; the betrayal of her French boyfriend; all the pain she'd caused her family; her mother's cold-hearted attitude over many years.

'Okay, mom,' said Laura, ending the call.

She sat on the edge of the bed, staring out of the hotel window.

'I killed my daddy,' she whispered to herself.

She grabbed her bag and left the hotel, driving to the nearest diner – the traditional American sort with red-leather furniture and stale coffee. The air was thick with the smell of fry-ups and the booming voices of working men at rest. She took a seat at a table and stared into space.

A teenage waitress approached. Her hair was dyed red and her sleeveless t-shirt showed off two well-toned arms, one of which was tattooed with her boyfriend's name. She was chewing gum manically as she addressed Laura.

'Hello love. What can I get you?'

Laura woke up with the word 'love' and gazed at the fine, youthful face.

'Coffee please, black.'

The waitress hurried behind the counter, filling a mug with a filtered brew. Laura took a sip and grimaced at the weak slop that passed for coffee in American diners. She longed for the espressos of Paris and Buenos Aires.

'Would you like something to eat?'

'No thanks,' Laura whispered.

The waitress – a girl with a kind nature – stood for a moment looking at her customer.

'Are you okay?'

Laura suddenly felt the need to open up, even to a stranger. After all, strangers were a safer bet. They would never meet again, and some human contact seemed of critical importance just then.

'I've lost my father and my lover all in one go,' said Laura.

The waitress laid a gentle hand on Laura's shoulder.

'That's pretty tough. I feel sorry for you. But listen, you're still alive and that's what matters. Just don't give up!'

Laura raised her eyebrows at hearing such encouraging advice from such a young woman, the words of a *femme sage* issuing from a teenage waitress.

'No, I won't give up. I've waited a long time to find the love of my life, and I don't plan to lose him just like that.'

Chapter 16
Poison in the Well

In a mud-brick hut in the middle of a desert oasis, a handful of men sat around a charcoal burner. A large bronze coffee pot sat above the glowing embers, and from the spout wafted a glorious, reviving scent. The brew would be much appreciated by the assembled company, who would need to keep their minds sharp in the coming hour or so.

On the floor of the hut, close against the walls, were arranged rows of cushions, with more serving as back-rests. Ali and Ma sat cross-legged, flanked by their hosts, watching closely as a boy lifted the pot and began to serve coffee to each man in turn. Once everyone had been served, they sipped at the scalding liquid, uttering murmurs of appreciation.

Ali was in heaven; it was not often that he tasted fresh-ground Bedouin coffee like this, complete with fresh cardamom seeds. Ma, meanwhile, was not so impressed – but he managed to keep his feelings to himself.

The group chatted politely for a while, passing the time before the much-anticipated arrival of the tribe's chief – a man named Rajab – at which point the serious discussions would start in earnest. Ali was not, of course, used to being kept waiting, but this was the last tribe on his list, and he was inclined to be patient. Added to which, the chief's tardiness was due to a hospital appointment, which was a better excuse than most. Age brought wisdom, but also certain physical limitations, diabetes being one of them.

Seated to Ali's right was Idris, the plump *jihadist* who had mentored the young Abdul prior to his bloody sacrifice in a family restaurant. Idris was at the meeting with a friend from the *madrasa*, and they were full of self-importance. They had never before escorted so valuable a VIP as Ali, and they felt the occasion was a sign of their growing status.

Of course, Idris felt nothing but contempt for Ali's well-publicized, un-Islamic lifestyle: the prostitutes, the gambling, the alcohol. Added to which, Idiris and his fellow *jihadists* were of the view that the nation's wealth had been largely squandered by the ruling elite, which meant Ali and his extended family, including Lolowa and Prince Yousef.

So far as Idris was concerned, they were all as bad as each other. Nothing would change for the better until a revolution had been enacted – an Islamic revolution that would sweep away all corruption and debauchery in one go. The problem was, of course, that accomplishing such a goal was likely impossible without some influential friends in high places, members of the ruling elite with whom to form an alliance. Perhaps Ali and his clique were the route to success – perhaps not.

The elders updated Ali on the current mood in Jawhar, while Ma listened, ever mindful of the minimal contribution from Idris. Why was this plump young man looking so serious? Why was there the hint of a sneer on his mouth as he listened in silence?

Ma watched Ali too as he conversed with the more vocal elders. The prince looked generally at ease, although his frailty was evident through his white silken robes. The Chinese spy wondered if he was the only one to notice the prince's weight-loss and the haggard face.

More and more men of all ages arrived at the tiny oasis, filing cautiously into the room. '*As-Salaamu Alaikum*,' they said, offering bows to Ali and then taking their seats. Some kissed each other four times on the cheeks, glad to catch up with other members of the tribe who they only saw on occasion.

The older men seemed reserved and respectful, chatting quietly amongst themselves, or else listening in on Ali's comments. But some of the younger men seemed to be lacking manners, sharing private jokes and engaging in banter. There was a lot of testosterone in the room, thought Ma.

Finally, Rajab arrived. Everyone stood up as he entered the room, including Ali, and the two men embraced like long-lost brothers. Rajab was a good fifteen years older than the prince, and with his health problems, he was far from spritely. Ma had seen several Bedouin chiefs in recent weeks, and Rajab would be the last. He was also the most hesitant, hardly exuding calm confidence. Indeed, Ma could not remember one chief in the past weeks who *had* inspired great confidence.

Rajab took his seat, accepted his cup of coffee and began to address the secret gathering.

He started by announcing his unswerving loyalty to Ali, an assertion that he hoped would bring him both strength and prestige.

'Brothers and family members, let us welcome our prince, our crown, our guide on the route to freedom. Let us offer him our hospitality and our service, as I do today. And join me in pledging your loyalty to our great leader in the difficult days that lie ahead. As you will know by now, the prince is seeking to return to power by way of a bloodless coup, and I for one offer him my full support. I pray for a smooth transition of power and a long and prosperous reign for the rightful ruler of our nation.'

The words were an enormous boost to Ali's self-esteem, which had grown increasingly shaky in the past weeks.

Rajab continued: 'Jawhar is being ruined and our people slaughtered by the current rulers and their foreign backers. We have great wealth, and everyone wants to steal it.'

The chief paused and looked around the room, his eyes lingering momentarily on Ma, who looked down in embarrassment.

'But under the leadership of Prince Ali,' continued Rajab, 'all such crimes will be at an end. We will do good business with the world and the money will be spent wisely. There will be justice and an end to poverty. We Bedouin will also be treated with the fairness that we deserve.'

Ali bowed his head in acknowledgement of Rajab's expression of support. He was aware, however, that the chief's motives were not entirely altruistic. Beneath all the patriotism and goodwill, Rajab was hoping for a slice of the cake, a personal share of the wealth to which the royal family had ready access.

Before Ali could respond with any expression of thanks, Idris piped up, breaking the protocol for such gatherings.

'The problem that must be addressed is the theft of our wealth by those in power. For many years, the ruling families have done business with other nations, working hand-in-hand with the enemy at our expense. This situation must be corrected if we are to fix the nation's problems.'

Idris was looking at Ali as he spoke, and the implied challenge was clear. The young *jihadist* was not afraid though, nor was he alone. The friend sitting beside him nodded and murmured in agreement, as did some of the other young men in the room.

Rajab opened his mouth to speak, but before he could do so, Idris continued: 'We need to build an Islamic state, a caliphate that will bring back the glories of the old times. We need to institute true Islam, to apply the *sharia* fully, crushing debauchery, prostitution and other evils. We must ban alcohol, for one thing, as this is among the greatest evils. Unless we do so, there will be no end to corruption, and all our efforts will be wasted.'

The young men murmured more loudly this time, a few uttering '*Allahu Akbar!*'

Anxious to reassert his control, Rajab stepped in: 'We are not blood-thirsty people. We want a peaceful society based on fairness, with all resources divided equally among the people. We must impose Islamic *sharia*, of course, following the example of the Prophet Mohamed – may the peace and blessings of Allah be upon him. But this must be achieved with a minimum of violence. Chaos and murder must be avoided at all costs.'

His plea was an impassioned one, and many were convinced. However, Idris and his young friends were not.

'No, we have to fight!' said Idris, jumping to his feet. 'Violent *jihad* is the only way forward. If it takes guns and bombs to achieve our goals, then so be it. We are ready for anything!'

Some of the young men applauded and there were more shouts of '*Allahu Akbar!*'

Ali waited patiently for the noise to die down. As he did so, he pondered the implications of this rowdy *jihadist* strain within the tribe. What did they hope to gain from a campaign of violence? Ali's plan involved a few arrests and a few sackings, the replacement of one prince with another. This much had already been made clear. The only death that was absolutely necessary was that of Lolowa. There was certainly no need for guns and bombs going off around the country; indeed, this was one thing he was seeking to stop.

Added to which, if the Chinese were to be kept onboard, the threat of violent *jihad* must be avoided at all costs. The prince glanced sideways at Ma, who was looking pale and serious. Clearly, the idea of a caliphate established by religious extremists did not sit well with him. His masters in Beijing were interested in Jawhar's natural resources – not getting embroiled in an Islamist insurgency.

Ali pondered his next utterances carefully. As a general rule, he preferred to say as little as possible. But he realized that the current situation was different; he must assert his dominance or risk failure. He recalled the oratory lessons he'd taken from a famous Egyptian journalist many years ago, a man who had written speeches for several Arab leaders.

Finally, he cleared his throat and began to speak: 'My fellow countrymen, we need to save our nation. We as individuals may come and go, but the nation remains forever. Yes, I have sinned and I confess this openly. I have indulged in alcohol and other evils, and I have gone astray. But I ask God for forgiveness and for the strength to take the true path once more. I also call upon the members of this tribe to put their trust in me as a man of God and of the people. If you will put your trust in me, then we will go forward together, as one, united in our common destiny.'

There was a burst of applause and the elders hailed Ali as their leader. Even some of the youngsters joined the applause, forgetting for the moment that Idris had called on them to oppose the corrupt, beer-swilling elite – of which Ali was a prime example.

Rajab joined the wave of enthusiasm, raising his fist in the air and shouting: 'We are all with you, Prince Ali. God save the prince!'

The room was soon alive with the same refrain, shouted in unison: 'God save the prince! God save the prince! God save the prince!'

Idris and his friend, however, did not join the chorus. Rather, they sat in silence, staring at Ali and Ma with great hostility.

'Perhaps we will follow you, Prince Ali, if you get treatment for your alcoholism and stop spending our money on prostitutes.'

The room fell silent, all eyes on the prince. According to tradition, a prince would be quite within his rights to kill a man on the spot for such insolence.

Ma leaned close to Ali – who was fuming – and whispered in his ear: 'Tread very carefully, Your Highness. We must not escalate these tensions. You have agreed already to mend your ways. Leave it there.'

Ali listened in silence, nodding in ascent, his hands folded in his lap. He knew exactly what he wanted to say to this young hoodlum Idris – but he bit his tongue instead.

Rajab clapped his hands and ordered the boy to pour more coffee. As the ancient ritual was enacted once more, the tensions seemed to subside, and the room was filled with friendly chatter. Ali enquired about Rajab's health, and he got a long explanation in reply – involving numerous doctors, nurses, tests and treatments. The prince almost wished he hadn't asked.

While this was going on, Idris and his friend rose from their seats and left, not bothering to offer parting wishes to their superiors. Several young men likewise left the room. They could be heard getting into their trucks and driving away.

Ma began to arrange alternative transport for the journey back to their accommodation, and pretty soon everyone was outside, standing by their vehicles, exchanging hugs and farewell wishes.

Rajab took Ali to one side and spoke quietly: 'My prince, are you quite sure you know what you're doing? Some of the people around you are not reliable, particularly these foreigners. They offer their support when it suits them but will drop you like a bag of potatoes once they've got what they want. Why not go back to South America or Europe and spend the rest of your life in peace?'

Ali was silent for a while, looking down at the old man's wrinkled hands, which were clasped around his own in friendship. Tears welled up in his eyes.

'My dear Rajab, I appreciate your concern and your kindness. But I must go through with this. You have no idea of the humiliation that I've suffered. If nothing else, I must do this for the sake of my pride.'

'May God be with you,' said Rajab, enfolding Ali in his embrace.

Ali knew the true meaning of these words: 'Only God can help you now.'

Before long, Ma and Ali were in the back of a Land Rover, speeding down a highway toward their safe-house, a holiday home by the sea. Both men were deep in thought, pondering the chances of success, which looked more remote now than ever. None of the Bedouin tribes had been overwhelmingly supportive, due in large part to their fear of Lolowa and her faction. Now there was the disruptive element represented by Idris and his group of *jihadist* insurgents. There was no telling how much influence their network had with the various tribes. The difficulty was in knowing whether the threat should be neutralized before the coup or afterwards. Both options posed serious risks – and the orders from Beijing were to proceed only if the risks of failure could be kept to an absolute minimum.

'I will have to speak with Beijing,' said Ma at last. 'They will want a full update on today's meeting. I can use the satellite phone when we get back.'

'Is there really much point?' asked Ali.

'Well, I don't think they'll be very enthusiastic,' admitted Ma. 'They really insist on zero risk, and Idris is very volatile. We might be making matters worse by forming an alliance with him.'

Ali was silent, looking from the window as the car sped through a little windswept village in the middle of nowhere.

'So what are you saying, exactly, Ma? Will you be leaping from the sinking ship?'

'The final decision is not mine to make, Your Highness, but...'

'Yes?'

'But I cannot strongly recommend the continued involvement of my government – at least not under the current circumstances.'

'I see,' said Ali.

The two men sat in silence until they finally arrived at the remote seaside villa, where the gate was opened by an armed guard. Ali and Ma were dropped in the courtyard and the Bedouin driver sped away, glad to put distance between himself and a doomed man.

Ali walked to the patio and took a seat in the shade. The houseboy came out with lemonade and ice, pouring two glasses for the returning travellers.

Ma, however, didn't join the prince. Rather he retrieved his satellite phone and walked into the garden, dialing a number as he went.

Ali downed a glass of lemon squash, wishing with every fibre of his being that it was a gin and tonic. A minute later, Ma returned, taking a seat at the table and looking more serious than ever.

'Well, what's the answer?' demanded Ali.

'I'm sorry, Your Highness, but we must leave Jawhar immediately. My instructions are to suspend the operation. We might take another look at the situation in the future, but for now, my government will not give the green light.'

Ali lit a cigarette and blew smoke into the early evening sky. As he watched the sun sinking toward the horizon, he thought of Laura and the life they might have had together in Argentina – and which they might still have somewhere, if only he could give up on this mad project of his.

'Oh, how I miss her!' he whispered to himself.

'Please, Your Highness, let us collect our belongings now and leave the country. We will be safe across the border by midnight, and tomorrow we can fly elsewhere. Then we will review the situation. But we should leave tonight. Ideally, we should leave immediately.'

Ali smiled, showing his pearly-white teeth, and tapped the back of Ma's hand.

'Not to worry, my good man. It is my fight. I have to go on.'

Ma's eyes were filled with tears. He was heartbroken to leave Ali like this – just at the critical moment.

'Your Highness...' he began.

'Leave, Ma, I insist. You are free of your obligations. Leave now and have a safe journey. I will not discuss it any further.'

The pair rose to their feet and embraced. Then Ma went to his room and packed his bags. Within an hour, he was in the back of a 4x4, crossing the border the same way he'd arrived, – bumping along some desert track in the cover of darkness.

Meanwhile, Ali sat on the patio as the sky darkened, smoking his way through a packet of cigarettes. If he'd had a bottle of booze in the house, he surely would have opened it straight away. Instead, he sipped on tea and blew smoke rings into the air, conjuring the image of Laura's smiling face before him.

The houseboy turned on the patio lights, but Ali scolded him, telling him to turn them off again. Ali wanted to sit in darkness; somehow Laura's face shone more brightly in the dark.

Chapter 17
A Friend in Need

Another bomb had gone off in the little emirate on the other side of the world, and the news channels were covering it like crazy, complete with images of blood-soaked streets and ambulances racing around. With dozens killed, the event was making headlines on Fox, CNN, MSNBC – and just about everywhere else.

Middle East experts had been invited to share their views, and all agreed that the rise of radical Islamist groups in the region was a worrying phenomenon. The Arab Spring had offered them an opportunity to spread their wings, filling the power vacuum by way of insurgency. In this particular emirate, said the experts, the *jihadists* had thus far been prevented from taking power – but this didn't stop them conducting an ongoing campaign of terror. What was needed was firm action, and the United States had a duty to contribute to the solution, offering advice and support to the emirate's current rulers. Military intervention might also be necessary at some point, if things got out of hand.

Laura was watching all of this from her bed at the Four Seasons Hotel in New York. Her high-rise room on Manhattan's 57th Street was the last word in modern luxury, but she was hardly able to enjoy it. The evening news was too disturbing, and her personal troubles hung over her like a cloud. Even a couple of large gin and Slimline tonics had failed to help her unwind.

She had flown out to meet an old friend named Cybil, an experienced newspaper journalist specializing in human rights issues. They had been firm friends in high-school, and the bond had survived both Laura's education in France and her chosen profession. Laura was in need of guidance, advice and reassurance, and there was nobody better qualified than Cybil.

As she sipped on her drink, Laura turned over the events of recent months, nurturing a growing sense of betrayal. She had been misguided by certain people in US intelligence, not least of all her contact in Buenos Aires. She felt used and abused – just as she'd been used and abused throughout her life, in both personal and professional capacities.

The CIA had used her to extract information on Ali's intentions and capabilities, and this had most likely been used against him. For all she knew, the information had been passed to Ali's enemies back home, who had no doubt been setting a nasty trap. Perhaps the trap had already been sprung.

On reflection, Laura could see that she'd also unknowingly acted as a vehicle for certain messages intended for Al's ears. All that chatter at US Embassy parties had been meant to reassure him of his popularity with his people, and the certainty that he'd be welcomed home with open arms. Laura had soaked up these upbeat messages and passed them along to Ali, unwittingly encouraging him in his suicidal venture.

How could she have been so naïve?

Now the spooks were done with her, having implemented their plan to secure US interests in Jawhar. It was the old imperial game: set the two sides fighting and do a deal with whichever comes out on top.

The question of her father's death was still unresolved, but she was convinced that this had also been the work of spooks. Whether they were US spooks or those of another nation was not clear, but they clearly wanted her out of the way for some reason. If only Jimmy Mitchell would get back to her with some sort of update…

She knocked back her gin and tonic and poured another. She was humiliated and angry, but not quite defeated – not yet.

'I will *not* let anyone stand between us,' she muttered to herself.

Her smartphone started to ring, belting out the tango tune that she adored, a melody to which she and Ali had danced. She answered and heard Cybil's voice, which had been lent a somewhat rough, masculine tone by years of heavy smoking.

'Sweetie, what are you doing in the Big Apple? I've miss you!'

'I've missed you too, Cybil, very much,' said Laura, a slight catch in her voice. 'Listen, I want to see you right away. I need to discuss something.'

'What's going on?' said Cybil. 'I thought you were living happily ever after in South America with your Prince Charming?'

'Not anymore! I don't even know where he is. I've lost my prince. He's the victim of a conspiracy – or we both are – and it's horrible. I can't take it anymore, Cybil!'

Laura was a little surprised by the emotion in her voice. She glanced at the bottle of gin, which stood half empty on the nightstand.

'Laura, you poor thing! I'm so sorry!'

'Yes, it's dreadful … and I don't know what to do.'

'I'm sorry I haven't been around for you. I've been so wrapped up in work – as always. We should definitely meet soon. Maybe tomorrow, if you like.'

'Yes please,' said Laura. 'That would be great.'

Cybil had indeed been busy in recent years, delving into human rights abuses arising from the so-called 'War on Terror'. She'd found the work fascinating and important, but it had taken its toll on the social front. She felt horribly guilty about losing touch with Laura. Now was the time to make up for it.

'Your hotel's pretty close to Central Park. We should meet in a coffee shop nearby. We used to hang out there all the time, if you remember, discussing our plans and dreams and all that stuff?'

'I certainly do. That would be great.'

'Okay, so let's say Caffè Storico at 1pm tomorrow?'
'Sounds great.'
'See you there.'

And Cybil was gone, in a rush as usual. Laura liked to pull her leg about her multi-tasking mania, calling her Miss Perpetuity. Cybil always took it well.

Laura was glad to have a trusty ally at last. Even so, she would have to kill another evening alone in her suite, battling to keep the dark thoughts at bay. She rose from the bed and stepped over to the neat little coffee machine, making a double espresso with lots of sugar. Settling on the sofa, she clicked through the TV channels in search of something distracting, but nothing took her fancy. She returned to her phone and checked WhatsApp and Facebook, finding that her friends in France were all getting on with their lives pretty much as normal. Some of them seemed quite happy. She trawled through the photographs of her father's funeral, which had been plastered across social media. There she was, standing by the graveside, too shocked to cry.

She typed Ali's name into a search engine and scanned the internet for news of his movements; finding none, she scrolled through endless photos from previous years, showing him at public events, entering or leaving buildings, giving speeches and smiling to crowds of onlookers. She lingered particularly on press photos of the two of them together, snapped in the streets of London and Buenos Aires. She had never seen these images before, and she found them haunting somehow, like images of long-dead relatives.

Finally, she logged off and poured another stiff drink, flopping on the bed and staring at the ceiling. She drifted back two decades to her youth in New York. After graduating from high-school, she and Cybil had volunteered on projects to help poor immigrants with their applications for US residency. They would take their lunch breaks together, eating hotdogs in the park or munching on sandwiches in local cafes. They had no idea how their lives might turn out, but it all seemed fresh and exciting and hopeful – the hopefulness of youth.

They developed a special relationship that had endured, despite their taking different directions in life. Being a talented linguist, Laura won a scholarship to study at the Sorbonne, then continued to graduate studies in Montpellier. Finally, she began her lucrative career as a provider of comfort to wealthy men. Cybil, meanwhile, remained in New York and studied journalism. She then launched upon a successful newspaper career, mixing with the political elites while somehow maintaining her integrity. Indeed, she made a name for herself as an investigative reporter specializing in revealing political and financial corruption. In the end, she'd been drawn to human-rights issues, particularly where they related to the foreign policy – which was very often.

In fact, this specialism was one reason that Laura thought Cybil might be able to help. Cybil had a lot of great connections, both in government agencies and the world of foreign-policy reporting. Some of them were Middle East specialists, and Cybil could rely on them to do a little delving on her behalf. Laura knew it was a big ask – and she didn't want to get Cybil in trouble – but she knew the girl would come through.

As her eyelids started to close, she wondered if she should just drop everything and fly out to Jawhar in search of Ali. Perhaps fate and the power of their love would throw them together somehow?

The next morning she awoke with a mild hangover. The bedside clock said 11am. If she wanted to meet Cybil on time, she'd have to get moving. She had room service deliver coffee and croissants and soon started to feel more human. She then showered, combed her long blond hair and dressed hurriedly: Calvin Cline Jeans, a crumpled t-shirt and an Italian leather jacket smelling of luxury.

She called reception and ordered a taxi then rushed downstairs like Cinderella fleeing from a ball. She jumped into the taxi and gave directions to the café. The driver was amused by the destination, which was easily walkable. Rich people would spend hours in the gym to lose a few pounds, but they refused to stroll the length of Central Park.

On entering the stylish Caffè Storico, Laura was greeted by the head waiter. She ignored him and stalked over to Cybil, who was sipping from a café latte and checking the news on her phone. Cybil stood up and the two embraced.

'How are you doing, honey?' asked Cybil.

Laura buried her face in her friend's shoulder and began to sob, her tears soaking into the white cotton t-shirt.

'Shhhh...' said Cybil, rocking gently. 'Take it easy, sweetheart. Take it easy.'

Cybil was concerned for Laura, but she was also embarrassed. Several customers were giving them curious looks. She helped Laura to a seat and sat next to her, one arm around her shoulders. Laura took a few moments to wipe her nose and catch her breath. She swallowed and cleared her throat.

'You've got to help me, Cybil. I don't know what I'm doing. I've never been so terrified in my life.'

Cybil was listening attentively, eyes drinking in every clue. Laura thought for a moment she looked like a psychotherapist sizing up a new patient, trying to determine whether this one was bat-shit crazy.

'You know me very well, Cybil,' continued Laura, trying to sound a bit more normal. 'I'm not prone to breakdowns or anything like that. I've been through a lot over the years, and I've always kept a level head.'

'I know, honey. You're very strong.'

'I mean, I've had some strange and dangerous clients. Some of them were powerful people too, famous, well connected. They screwed me, spat on me, tortured me – you name it. But that was really nothing compared to what I'm going through now. I've never felt pain like this before.'

The head waiter arrived, looking a little put out. Cybil ordered two glasses of red wine and the waiter disappeared again.

'Go on, Laura.'

'Well, like I said, that was all tough, but it was nothing compared to this. I finally found the love of my life. I wanted to settle down with him and make a fresh start, raise children and make a home, just like normal people. Ali's a prince, of course, but he's human, just like anyone else. He'd make a wonderful father.'

'I'm sure he would.'

'But now it seems like it was just a mirage. The closer I got to Ali, the more distant he became. I mean, I was ready to settle down, to commit fully, but there was always some doubt in his mind. He always thought he might go back home and take control again, regain his throne...'

'He hasn't gone back, has he?'

Cybil was genuinely shocked. Up to this point, she hadn't really understood the gravity of the situation. She thought that perhaps Ali and Laura had split up, but she hadn't realized that he'd gone on a mission to regain power – to conduct a coup d'état.

'I don't know for sure, Cybil, but I think he may have gone home. If so, it would be a coup, and I've no idea if he'd be a success. It's very dangerous, of course. I haven't spoken to him for three weeks; he won't answer the phone. I spoke with the hotel in Buenos Aires, but they say he checked out the day after I arrived in the States. I honestly do think he's gone home.'

Laura blew her nose again, and the waiter arrived with the wine. The two women waited in silence as he set the glasses down, bowed very slightly and departed. Laura could feel herself on the verge of tears again. She reached for her wine and gulped it down in one go. How ironic, she thought, after spending so much time trying to convince Ali to give up the booze!

Cybil didn't touch her wine. She was silent, watching. If she was going to be dragged into all this, she wanted a clear head.

'So you've got no idea of his movements since you left Argentina?'

'None at all.'

'Did he actually say that he was planning a coup d'état?'

'Well, he was always hinting at it, and he had a lot of secretive meetings. I knew something was happening, but I suppose he didn't want to involve me. And then the moment I came back to the States, he was gone. I don't know what route he'd take, but I assume he'd have to be pretty secretive.'

'I suppose he could fly to the Middle East by private jet and then cross the desert by jeep,' suggested Cybil. 'I imagine he's got lots of contacts still, members of the military and intelligence who are loyal to him.'

'Oh, he's got lots of friends, I'm sure,' said Laura, he voice heavy with sarcasm. 'It's just that I'm no longer one of them… apparently.'

Cybil took Laura's hand in both of hers.

'Listen, Laura. You've got to be strong. Whatever Ali's doing, I'm sure it's due to his sense of duty to his country. It doesn't mean he doesn't love you. Obviously he loves you. I can see how close you were just by how much you're hurting. You've had a few relationships in your time, but I can see this is the real thing. It's like watching Madame Butterfly!'

Laura laughed at this. She's never thought of herself as the dramatic type, but she could see how it looked from the outside.

'Listen, I'll do my best to help you,' said Cybil, allowing herself a sip of wine at last. 'I know a few people who may have information: people in intelligence, the Foreign Service, Middle East journalists, that sort of thing. I'll make a few discrete enquiries and see if anyone has knowledge of his movements. There are ways of tracking people.'

'Thanks, Cybil.'

'That's alright. But I must warn you against going out there, Laura. Don't go running after him, because no power on earth could protect you if you fell into the hands of the ruling family. I don't know what they'd do to you, but it wouldn't be nice. The US government wouldn't lift a finger to save you, I can promise you that much. They're only concerned about their own interests.'

'I just want to be with him…' said Laura, collapsing once more in tears.

Cybil held her friend in her arms, her face buried in Laura's messy hair.

'Come on, girl. Be strong.'

Laura sat upright and blew her nose again.

'I'm sorry,' she said. 'I just can't seem to keep it together. It's all just been so horrible. And it's not just Ali. I think my Dad was murdered.'

'Murdered? I thought he was hit by a car.'

'That's what they say, but I think it was deliberate – just to get me out of the way. He never walked anywhere in town. If he had an appointment, he'd drive there. He had a bad hip, so walking wasn't exactly his favourite pass-time.'

'Right, I see. But who would have done that?'

'Well… it could be anyone, I suppose. Maybe someone who wanted to get me out of the way so that Ali could disappear… I really don't know.'

Cybil was looking very serious now. The gravity of the situation was slowly sinking in. She was also worried for Laura, not just her emotional wellbeing, but her safety.

'Laura, I think you should stay off the streets for a while. Don't go walking around, okay?'

'Why not?'

'Just for your own safety. You never know. Stay inside for the next week or two, and don't trust anyone, okay?'

'Okay.'

'Take a taxi back to the hotel and try to relax a bit. Watch some movies. I'll make a few calls this afternoon and then get in touch when I know something. Don't leave the hotel until you've heard from me personally.'

'Alright.'

The two friends left the café and went their separate ways. In the back of her cab, Cybil pulled out a throw-away mobile phone and dialled a number.

'Hello. It's me.'

'Well, this is a nice surprise.'

'Can we meet up? I need to pick your brains.'

Chapter 18
Company Business

Jimmy Mitchell looked at his Rolex watch. He was fifteen minutes early, but that wouldn't be held against him. He knocked and waited. Moments later, Mike Reynalds opened the door, looking dapper in blue pin-stripes, his bald head smooth and shiny.

'Hello Jimmy,' he said. 'Good to see you.'

'Good to see you too, Mike.'

The two men exchanged firm handshakes and entered the George Washington Suite.

'Take a seat, Jimmy, and I'll be right with you. There's coffee and nibbles. Help yourself.'

'Sure will.'

The two men sank into the comfortable armchairs either side of a marble-topped coffee table. Jimmy poured himself a coffee and bit into a Danish pastry. Mike was scrolling through his phone, engrossed in rearranging his diary. He was meeting some real high-rollers this week, some of them deep in organized crime. He was hoping the Sheikh wouldn't be too late, because there was another meeting this evening that absolutely could not be bumped.

Jimmy looked around the room. He'd been to this hotel before, but never in the George Washington Suite. He tended to think that all five-star hotels in DC were the same, but this one was particularly nice, with its classic décor, smart but understated.

'We may move to the dining room when the Sheikh arrives,' said Mike. 'He tends to bring half a dozen people to these little meetings: secretary, interpreter, someone to clip his toenails while he talks, someone else to light his cigars. You know the sort of thing.'

'Sure do. No problem at all.'

'I'm nearly done with my diary here, and then you'll have my full attention.'

Jimmy was glad to have a moment alone with Mike. He had a few questions for his colleague, and they were better discussed in private – as with all Company business.

'There,' said Mike, finally putting down the phone, 'I'm all yours.'

'Well, thanks for inviting me along to this meeting, Mike. I really appreciate it.'

'Not at all. You've been very helpful at your end. It's only right that you should see a bit more of the picture from our side. After all, we may want to call on you again in future.'

'That's music to my ears.'

Mike poured himself a fresh coffee and dropped in two sugars as he pondered his next statement.

'Now, you're a Latin America specialist, Jimmy, and I'm Middle East. As the old saying goes: 'East is East and West is West...' However, your work in Buenos Aires has certainly helped move things along in my area of operations. And I mean big time. We believe Prince Ali is now in-country, and thanks to you, we have a more detailed picture of his network.'

'Glad to be of service.'

'Of course, there are other elements of Operation Campfire that you'll be learning for the first time today, just as soon as the Sheikh arrives, but I thought I'd give you a heads-up. Now, this guy goes by several names, as one might expect. Today he's Sheikh Mostafa Al-Tawir. He's also known as Abu Said, and our operational codename for him is Fennec – which is a sort of crafty desert fox. Personally, I think that's a bit too flattering, but it wasn't my decision. You can just call him 'Your Excellency' when he arrives.'

'Is he royalty?'

'Not exactly, but he's from some aristocratic bloodline linked to the Prophet Mohamed, or something like that. So it's best to be respectful.'

'Will do.'

'Now, to give you some broad brush strokes, we're aiming to get some idea of how the *jihadist* threat is developing. If our assessments are correct, they will be moving into a new phase by early summer. At the moment it's just a low-level security issue, but they may be stepping that up considerably in the next month or so. The Sheikh has his own links to these groups – unofficially of course. But what it means is that he's able to provide us with up-to-date information on their movements and plans. He can also tell us the rough number of recruits and the sort of weaponry they have access to.'

'Are they well-armed at present?' said Jimmy.

'So far, it's been mostly small-arms and suicide vests. However, it seems they'll soon take delivery of heavy machine-guns, mortars, RPGs and a whole load of Toyota pick-up trucks. There have even been rumours of shoulder-launch anti-tank and anti-aircraft missiles. If that's true, then they'll be equipped for a full-scale insurgency. That's what we're looking to find out. Our planning rather depends on this information – and on the insurgency taking place, of course.'

'How reliable is this guy's information?'

'He's very well plugged in. Aside from his powerful political and business contacts, he spends a lot of time with senior *mukhabarat* people from around the Gulf. That's 'Arab intelligence' to you. Added to which, he's personal friends with the guys who supply the weapons – which is about as close as you can get without actually getting splattered with blood.'

'So he doesn't go to training camps?'

'He's never been to a training camp in his life, and he probably never will. As I say, he has a personal manicurist travelling with him wherever he goes. The closest this Sheikh ever got to roughing it was taking a taxi when his limo broke down.'

'Okay, so he's pretty hands-off.'

'Yes, but he's *really* good. Thanks to his various friends, we can expect some serious fireworks in the coming months. And we should have some advance warning. But, of course, you didn't hear that from me.'

'Yes, of course.'

'And today's meeting never happened, right?'

'Absolutely.'

Mike's phone rang. He checked the number and picked up.

'Hello. Sure, we're all ready.'

He hung up and turned back to his colleague.

'The Sheikh is in the building. He's a little bit early for once. I guess he ran out of things to buy.'

'Big spender then?'

'You wouldn't believe it. Last time we met, he arrived with two million dollars in jewellery that he'd just picked up on Connecticut Avenue. I'm told he's buying up real-estate in Argentina too, so you'd better watch out.'

'Really?'

'Oh sure, when nuclear war starts, he'll be sitting in a bunker in Patagonia.'

'Well, if you've got the money, why not?'

'My thoughts exactly. Now, was there anything else you wanted to discuss before he arrives?'

Jimmy had a number of questions on his mind, but one seemed most pressing: what to do about Laura Sanders. He had a gut instinct, but he wanted confirmation from his colleague.

'I've been contacted again by Laura Sanders,' he said.

'She's in the States now, I understand.'

'That's right. You'll have heard about her father, of course. Apparently, he's dead.'

'Yes, that had come to my notice.'

'Well, she's keen to know who might have been responsible. She asked me to find out.'

'And what did you say?'

'I didn't have a chance to say anything. She just hung up.'

'Well, we don't know who did it, actually. It wasn't anyone in the Company, that's for sure.'

'Could it be an enemy of Prince Ali?'

'Perhaps, but they'd have nothing to gain, so far as I can tell.'

'Could it be the Chinese?'

'It's a reasonable guess, but we can't be sure.'

'So what should I tell her?'

'Do you have to tell her anything?'

'Well, to be frank, I don't see any benefit in maintaining contact with the woman – unless you want me to keep on her on a string?'

'I think that if you were to cut that string and never speak with her again, that would be just fine. If we need anything else from Laura Sanders, we'll arrange it from our end.'

'That's exactly what I was hoping you'd say.'

'Anything else?'

'Nothing that can't wait.'

There was a knock at the door and the two men got to their feet, Mike striding over to open the door.

Two Arab security officers in kakhi suits and Ray Bans entered first, scouring the suite for danger. Moments later, the Sheikh stepped in, dressed in his white robes and a red-and-white checked headscarf. He seemed older than Jimmy had imagined, possibly in his sixties, though his pointy beard was jet black. As anticipated by Mike, the Sheikh was accompanied by half a dozen assistants. Two additional security guards stood watch in the corridor.

Mike and the Sheikh exchanged handshakes, kisses and greetings in Arabic, and finally Jimmy was introduced.

'This is my colleague and good friend Jimmy, who has been helping with some aspects of this project. Today he'll be joining us, just to get a better picture of what we do. That's assuming you have no objections, Your Excellency?'

The Sheikh's interpreter translated.

'No problem,' said the Sheikh, showing off one of his few English phrases and shaking Jimmy's hand warmly.

Soon they were settled comfortably around the dining table, with hotel staff delivering fresh coffee, juice, water, fruit, dates and canapés. To Jimmy's amusement, one of the Sheikh's assistants prepared a cigar for his boss.

Mike turned to Jimmy and spoke softly: 'Forgive me if we dive into Arabic from this point on. It's just quicker than translating everything. If there's anything important that you need to know, I'll translate or just fill you in later.'

'No problem at all.'

The meeting got under way, with Mike and the Sheikh exchanging greetings and asking after each other's wives and families. Soon, though, they were down to business, and Jimmy wished for the first time in his life that he'd accepted the CIA's offer of Arabic-language training. He made a mental note to take a course some time.

As he listened to the chatter, the only words he could recognize were Arabic names: Mostafa, Mahmoud, Ali, Yousef and Idris. That last name in particular seemed to be mentioned quite a lot.

After a while, Mike leaned close to Jimmy and whispered: 'I'll tell you all about Idris after the meeting. He's turning out to be a real super-star.'

Chapter 19
The Gates of Hell

'The gates of Hell seem to have opened wide,' said the US ambassador, stubbing out his cigarette furiously. His personal assistant, Marion, stopped shuffling papers and stared. Thomas Carwell-Jones was generally liked as an ambassador, not least of all for his composure in a tight spot – but the strain was finally starting to show.

They were in the middle of arranging the evacuation of US citizens as the insurgents crept closer to the capital. Buses were taking people to the airport, which was thankfully still providing flights to destinations across the region. All of which seemed simple enough, but the situation was complicated by numerous American companies who had invested millions in Jawhar and were reluctant to cut their losses. It was the ambassador's job to soothe tempers and talk sense.

There was no denying that the situation was going downhill by the day. What had until recently been a terrorist problem had transformed into a widespread insurgency. Weapons were flooding into the country from somewhere, and foreign fighters had joined the *jihadist* cause, aiming for victory or a place in Paradise.

With little in the way of firm leadership, the government forces were on the back foot, losing village after village, town after town. Now there were reports of gunfire in the capital's leafy suburbs, and the national highways were closed to all but local traffic. The petroleum industry had ground to a standstill too, with dozens of workers shot where they stood. Any day now, the insurgents might be parking their pick-up trucks outside the embassy – and then it really would be over.

The government had been holding frantic discussions with various Western powers, pleading for logistical help, new military hardware, intelligence support, or at least an injection of sound advice. But help had been slow in arriving. The West seemed to be biding its time, unsure which way to jump. Should they back this crumbling regime, based around a corrupt, aging elite and run along tribal lines? Or should they back the insurgents, who showed great fighting spirit but had little experience in the business of running a country? If the US government had a definite plan, it was holding its cards close to its chest.

Carwell-Jones had been asking himself the same range of questions these past few months: which way would they be jumping? He was the man on the spot, of course, and he had all the right training to make such a decision. As a career diplomat and seasoned Arabist, he could have chosen a firm line back in 2011 and steered a sensible course, avoiding all this mayhem. But his orders ultimately came from Washington, DC, and his superiors seemed to be holding out to the very end.

Bearing in mind previous foreign-policy fiascos, he wasn't particularly surprised to be preparing to shred all the files. He only wished he'd been given permission to start the evacuation sooner. Would it be helicopters on the roof again?

Thankfully, his wife had already flown to Beirut with the children; they would be spending the summer holidays in California. The non-essential embassy staff were gone too; that was a load off his mind. He was grateful too for the continued presence of Marion, this plump, plucky New Yorker who had refused to leave his side. Foreign Service staff like her were worth their weight in gold.

The ambassador was jerked out of his thoughts by the red phone on his desk. He looked at Marion, who was gathering her papers in preparation for leaving the room. He shook his head, motioning for her to remain. She had come this far with him; she might as well listen to his red-phone calls from Washington. After all, maybe she could offer some advice.

'Ambassador Carwell-Jones speaking,' he said.

It was the Secretary of States' office, and the booming voice on the line belonged to someone who took US interests in the region very seriously.

'Yes, sir,' said the ambassador. 'Of course, I understand fully. Do we have a time-frame for the intervention?'

Marion watched her boss as he lit another cigarette. Was it her imagination, or was his hand shaking as he held the lighter?

'That's right, sir,' he continued. 'We have our regular intelligence briefing scheduled for 08:00 hours tomorrow morning. The Defense Attaché will be present, as will the CIA Station Chief. Will the admiral be able to make that meeting? Yes, of course, we can have everything laid on. The security team is on 24-hour standby, so we'll make arrangements.'

Marion returned to shuffling her papers. For the first time since this all began, she wondered whether she should have taken that offer of a flight out.

'Thank you, sir. Good bye,' said Jones.

As he hung up, the shock was evident on his face. He leaned back in his swivel chair and blew a big cloud of smoke. Marion stopped shuffling.

'Well, Marion, it seems a US Navy admiral, a Marine Corps colonel and a whole bunch of CIA officers will be dropping by for breakfast.'

'I see. What's the idea?'

'Well, nobody has seen fit to provide me with the details, but it seems somebody has big plans for this little country – big military plans.'

'Is the evacuation to continue?'

'Yes, until further notice. If anything, we should probably speed things up.'

The ambassador had just started to blow smoke rings when the telephone rang, this time not the red phone, thankfully.

'Shall I take that, sir?' said Marion.

'No, it's alright,' said Jones, lifting the receiver.

Pretty soon, he wished hadn't bothered. It was the personal secretary of Prince Yousef, his voice alternating between terror, hesitation and humiliation. He was begging the ambassador to save the situation, to come to the government's rescue. Wasn't there something the US military could do? The US Navy was anchored offshore, complete with a large contingent of marines and several F-16 aircraft. Would it be so difficult to intervene? Wasn't it the responsibility of the United States to prevent a massacre? Didn't the ambassador care about long-term ties and business interests?

Carwell-Jones was sympathetic, of course, but he didn't have permission to show it – and he was certainly not in a position reveal plans for a possible military intervention.

'What the hell are you thinking?' he said. 'I can't just order a military intervention. I'm here as the representative of the US government, and the policy of my government is to encourage a peaceful political resolution to the current crisis. The Secretary of State is aware of the situation and will act accordingly. I'm afraid these continual begging telephone calls will accomplish nothing. If the situation changes, you'll be the first to hear about it.'

And without waiting for a reply, the ambassador hung up. Marion has never known the ambassador to hang up like that. Things must be getting pretty bad.

* * *

The US embassy was not the only institution preparing to evacuate. Prince Yousef's palace was also a hive of activity, with staff at every level buzzing around, doing their best to maintain the appearance of calm. Servants were packing cases, carefully wrapping the most expensive and delicate objects: porcelain, paintings, jewellery, antique clocks, Persian rugs. Meanwhile, gold bars and wads of money were being packed into crates ready for transport. The first trucks were loaded and ready to go, although the drivers had no idea where they might be heading. Was anywhere in the country safe?

Yousef was in his private suite with his favourite wife, trying to console the children, who were in tears. Meanwhile, his chief of intelligence, Sheikh Fahman, was encouraging the prince to hurry up and finalise his plans for departure. A royal jet was ready at the air-force base, said Fahman, and there would be room for twenty people on board. Several foreign powers would be willing to provide sanctuary for the prince and his immediate family. But he must make his decision quickly, because the insurgents might break through at any moment. Yousef was listening but only half-heartedly; how could he concentrate on matters of state when his children were so upset?

Fahman's two deputies were also listening, mobile phones in their hands, ready to make the necessary telephone calls to set things in motion. They looked like frightened dogs, crouching at their master's feet.

Suddenly, the doors burst open and everyone looked up. It was Princess Lolowa, striding down the centre of the room with her trademark air of stern determination.

'What is wrong with you?' she demanded. 'Aren't there any real men in this country?'

Everyone was silent. Fahman stopped in mid-sentence, his mouth hanging open. Lolowa was simultaneously his cousin and his worst nightmare. She had opposed his appointment as head of intelligence, and no doubt she blamed him for the current state of chaos. He had long expected that she would hold him accountable, and now it seemed the time had come.

'You are completely useless, Fahman! I don't know how many millions of dollars we diverted your way, and you still haven't found Ali. There are rumours everywhere that he's still at large, plotting another coup. We've only just crushed one attempt, and now they say he's planning another one. You've rounded up hundreds of people in the past week, but it seems you can't get the one man that's most important. The media is full of such speculation, and it won't stop until you've brought me his dead body. Where is he?'

'Your Highness, please forgive me,' said Fahman, shaking like a leaf. 'We have tried everything; we have searched everywhere. But he is nowhere to be found. Where else should we look?'

'Well, have you checked your pockets?' replied the woman, her words dripping with sarcasm.

Fahman was silent, looking down at his shoes.

Lolowa continued: 'It seems I will have to take charge here, which is hardly a surprise. You will capture Ali and bring him back here, but you will do so by following my plan. Come with me.'

The ageing princess turned and walked from the room, Fahman following close behind. They walked down one flight of stairs to the first basement level and into the security complex, where security guards watched CCTV monitors and listened to radio chatter. At the far end of a corridor, a soldier stood to attention in front of a metal door.

Lolowa waved her hand and the soldier unlocked the door. Fahman followed the princess along another corridor and into a windowless office on the right. There before him, seated at a bare conference table, were two men of European appearance in smart suits. They stubbed out their cigarettes, smiling at Fahman and offering handshakes.

'These two gentlemen have flown all the way from Langley, Virginia, to offer their assistance,' said Lolowa. 'They have great expertise in sniffing out fugitives and trouble-makers, and they promise me that Ali will be captured within the week. Of course, they require access to all of your intelligence databases.'

Fahman opened his mouth as if to speak, but nothing came out.

'You see, gentlemen,' said Lolowa, 'I told you he would be cooperative.'

Chapter 20
A Helping Hand

Laura had not left her room for three days. She'd spent most of the time in her night-clothes, either sleeping or collapsed on the sofa, watching TV. She'd managed to limit her consumption of news and had focused instead on movie channels. She watched so many love stories and soppy dramas that her eyes were hurting. It didn't help that she'd been drinking heavily and dosing up on sleeping pills.

She was watching a stupid romantic comedy on Thursday afternoon when a note was shoved under the door. She left it for a while, assuming it was the room-cleaning service. When she finally roused herself from the couch an hour later, she was shocked to find a letter in Cybil's handwriting:

'Darling Laura,
I hope you're being strong and staying safe. I've met with one of my contacts, and he's pretty sure he can find some information for you. However, it will take a little time, apparently. He said he'll do whatever he can to help.
Right now, I have to go away for a few days. I'm spending a long weekend in Seattle. Yes, more work! When I get back, I'll update you on developments. And we can meet for drinks, of course.
Take care of yourself and don't do anything stupid.
Your friend,
Cybil'

Laura wasn't sure whether to be happy or crushed. It was good to hear that Cybil had been active, and that one of her expert contacts was at least on the case. But there was no certainty of success, and she'd have to wait until after the weekend to find out.

She scrunched up the letter and threw it in the bin. Stomping to the fridge, she pulled out a half-bottle of vodka and poured herself a large glass. She picked up the bottle of sleeping pills and tipped some into her hand. How easy it would be, she thought, to take the whole lot... and just end it.

She put the pills back, grabbed a tub of ice cream, and returned to the sofa. If she had to watch romantic movies all through the weekend, then that's what she would do.

The next morning was a bright one, the early summer sun pouring through the living-room windows. Laura had slept on the couch, and she felt awful. Her head was thicker than ever, and as she sat up, she felt slightly ill. Just as she was wondering whether a shower might improve things, she noticed another note on the carpet by the door. Perhaps Cybil had been back and delivered an update while she was asleep.

Laura picked up the manila envelope and tore it open. Inside were an American passport and a computer print-out. She opened the print-out and saw a list of scheduled flights to Jawhar, all of them departing from New York the next day. One flight, late in the afternoon, was circled in yellow highlighter. A note in the right-hand column said 'seats available'.

She flipped open the passport. There on the information page was a photograph of herself, very much like the photo in her existing passport. She blinked and looked again at the pristine front-cover of the passport, just to check that it wasn't her existing, dog-eared travel document. But no, this was definitely a brand-new passport.

She looked inside once more and found that, while the photograph was hers, the name was not. Instead, the passport holder was listed as Janet Springer, aged 45.

What on earth was this? What sort of person had the facility to create fake passports like this – and in the space of just a few days? Presumably, only government officials could get this sort of thing done so quickly; either that or some highly-competent criminals. She knew that Cybil was well connected, but she had really surpassed herself this time.

Then again, Cybil had specifically warned her against going to Jawhar. She would be the last person to facilitate such a journey – unless, of course, her secret contacts had convinced her otherwise. Perhaps they would be waiting at the airport to take Laura straight to Ali's hideout. On the other hand, it might be a wicked trap.

She reached for her phone and called Cybil's number. There was no answer, just a message to say that she was unavailable. Laura thought of leaving a message of her own, but decided against it. Did it really matter who was behind all this, so long as it got her closer to Ali?

She flicked through the passport and found only one entry. It was a tourist visa for Jawhar, valid for six months. The intention here was quite clear. And if she knew herself at all, she would be boarding that flight the next day.

Chapter 21
Nowhere to Hide

Ali was enjoying the hospitality of his loyal servant Nabhan, who had turned his home into a safe-house for the fugitive prince. The place was small but comfortable, located in a suburb of the capital. Here Ali was able to settle for a while in humble yet reassuring surroundings, all the while being close to the centre of power, within easy reach of whichever influential figures might still wish to pledge their allegiance. Rumour had it that some had been arrested, but there were likely others that remained at liberty.

Nabhan was a handsome man of African heritage, his dark skin serving as a reminder of the Arabian slave trade, a phenomenon now consigned to history. He wore long white robes, always impeccably clean and well ironed. Now in his mid-50s, his goatee beard was silver-grey, while his teeth shone like pearls.

During his years in service, Nabhan had attained a degree of seniority within the royal household. While his family background was far from exalted, the prince had promoted him above others, largely in recognition of the man's good character and unswerving loyalty. After Ali was ousted from power, the servant found himself expelled from the palace, but he maintained contact with others who supported the prince. Indeed, he became a key figure in the underground network of those wishing a return to former times. Had Ma's plan come to fruition, Nabhan would have been a major player in the coup, and one of the main beneficiaries of success. Unlike many of Ali's other supporters, however, Nabhan was not motivated by money or power, but by devotion to a good master, a man who he saw as honest and just.

Nabhan was apologetic to His Highness for the modesty of his home, with its simple fabrics and furnishings. The food was simple too, consisting mainly of rice and lamb, cooked slowly over a wood fire. The dish was well seasoned with spices, although Ali noted that the rice lacked the expensive Persian saffron that he adored.

As the dinner plates were cleared from the table, Ali slapped his servant on the back, a sign of gratitude for his hospitality and support. In the absence of Laura, he had been craving some personal attention, and now he was getting it. The servants at the seaside villa where he had stayed with Ma had been reliable enough, but hardly affectionate. Even the driver who had dropped Ali at Nabhan's house was less than friendly. During the entire two-hour drive, the man had hardly uttered a word.

Now Ali was alone with his most loyal friend, and it felt like coming home, albeit without the benefits of satellite television and a well-stocked bar. While he missed his creature comforts, there was something liberating about living such a modest life, and he was reminded of the relative simplicity of his childhood pleasures, when he would run barefoot through the dunes and swim in the sea.

He was particularly glad to wave goodbye to his armed Bedouin guards, whose presence he considered oppressive. They had offered to join the prince on his onward journey, but Ali had ordered them to stay behind. He would be far less conspicuous if he travelled alone. Dressed as a grubby old shepherd, he might pass among the shadows unnoticed.

In any case, he had his gold-plated pistol handy. And once he had made contact with his friends in the capital, there would be weapons enough to go round. There would be army battalions pledging their allegiance, not to mention the greater part of the security apparatus. Of this, he was quietly confident.

Ali's bed was a mattress on the roof terrace. He slept fitfully, dreaming of his deceased son, his first love and Laura. Sometimes, he would just gaze up at the stars, recalling the days when he had accompanied his father on gazelle-hunting trips into the desert.

It was on the fourth night, just before dawn, that he awoke to the sounds of a commotion in the house. There was a lot of shouting and banging, and the sound of boots running up and down the stairs. Nabhan could be heard arguing with someone at high volume, and then shots were fired. The servant briefly squealed in pain and then was silent.

Ali was now on his feet, pulling his *deshdasha* over his head and jumping into his shoes. He grabbed his small backpack and ran to the far end of the roof terrace, away from the door leading into the house. He crouched in the shadows and slipped his hand into the backpack, pulling out his pistol. He pulled back the slide, placing a round in the chamber, then released the safety lock. He tried to bring his breathing under control, to stop his hands shaking.

He looked at the door, hoping he might hear Nabhan's booming voice once more, but there were only the sounds of a house being turned upside down. Then there were rifle butts banging against the door, which Ali knew to be locked. How long the lock would hold, he had no idea.

Who had given him away? Could it be a member of Nabhan's family, eager to boast of their honoured guest? Perhaps the rumours had spread and someone had decided to collect the reward? Was it betrayal or just back luck?

He was in fight-or-flight mode, but fighting was clearly useless. He might shoot half a dozen soldiers, but there would be more. They would swarm around him like bees. Running for cover was the only option.

Ali looked up at the six-foot wall before him, beyond which was the neighbour's roof and possible freedom. Before his stroke, he would have managed such an obstacle with relative ease. Now, he wasn't so sure. He shouldered his backpack, then reached up and grabbed the top of the wall. He managed to hang on for a while, but despite a furious struggle, he just couldn't pull himself over.

Gasping for breath, he looked around and saw an old chair in one corner of the roof. He grabbed it and placed it up against the wall. Gingerly, he stood on the wooden seat, then placed his elbows on top of the wall; with all his might, he swung his right leg up... and over. With a grunt, he dropped onto the neighbour's roof, wondering if he'd done any permanent damage.

As he crouched in the darkness, he saw a middle-aged women and two children standing before him. They had heard the noise and come out to learn what was happening. After all, burglaries were not unknown in the area.

As they stood staring at each other, Ali noticed an expression of recognition spread over the woman's face. Her eyes widened and she began to smile.

'Your Highness! Prince Ali!' she said. Then, remembering her manners, she pulled her headscarf over her hair long, dark hair. She covered her nose and mouth also, leaving only her sparkling eyes uncovered.

'Shut up!' hissed Ali, walking quickly over and clutching her arm. 'What's your name?'

'Rabab, Your Highness,' said the woman, blushing.

In a flash, Ali remembered her as one of the cleaners in his palace. No doubt there were many of his former employees in the neighbourhood. He thanked his lucky stars that he had always been decent to the cleaners, tipping them generously ahead of religious holidays.

'Long live the Prince!' she whispered. 'God save the Prince!'

'Thank you, Rabab,' said Ali, 'but we must get inside right away. I'm in danger.'

She turned swiftly, grabbing her children by the arms and hurrying through the doorway. Ali followed, descending two flights of stairs to the ground floor. The woman ordered her children into the living room then led Ali through the kitchen and into the cellar. The place was pitch-black, and Ali feared he might trip and break his neck on the stone steps. Reaching the bottom, Rabab lit a candle revealing various crates and boxes, bottles of oil and cans of food, along with baskets of eggs and vegetables fresh from the market. Such cellars were common enough in the older houses, offering a cool retreat from the summer heat in the days before air-conditioning. It was also a suitable place to locate a well, such as that which now stood before Ali, covered with a circular lid formed of wooden planks.

Rabab drew the heavy lid to one side, revealing a cross beam and a metal bucket suspended from a sturdy rope.

'In here,' she said, pointing at the bucket.

Ali looked in amazement at the bucket then peered down into the watery depths of the old well. He couldn't see the bottom, but he caught a whiff of something rotten. Clearly the well was long out of use, perhaps serving as a watery grave for mice and spiders.

'I can't get in there,' he muttered. 'I'll fall down.'

'Your Highness, you have no choice. There's nowhere else to hide.'

There was a loud crashing sound upstairs and the children started to wail. Presumably the search party had burst into the house. They would find the cellar soon enough.

Ali climbed onto the circular stone wall, and grabbing the cross beam, slipped his feet into the bucket.

'I will lower it a couple of feet and then lock it,' said Rabab, turning the handle and applying the lock. 'It's safe now,' she said. 'It will take your weight, Your Highness. You can trust me.'

Ali didn't entirely trust either Rabab or the bucket, but he clearly had no choice. The wooden cover was dragged into position over his head and everything went dark. He heard the woman piling boxes and broken chairs on top of the cover and then shifting other objects around the room. He hung on tight to the cross beam, trying to moderate his breathing as his lungs filled with the stale air. He wondered how far he would fall if the cross-beam gave way – and whether his landing would be soft.

In the kitchen, an army captain was shouting at Rabab's mother, who had been roused from her bed. The old woman was yelling back at him. Didn't he have any sense of decency? Did he always burst in on women when their sons and husbands were away? Didn't the captain have a wife and daughters of his own?

The captain shoved her aside and yanked open the door to the cellar, ordering two soldiers down the steps with a torch. As they embarked on their mission, Rabab came up the steps with a tray of eggs. The soldiers pushed past her and she dropped the eggs, cursing at their clumsiness.

'What will my children eat for breakfast now?' she screamed.

The soldiers shone the torch around and began kicking boxes by way of a cursory search. Then one spotted the well and was clearly thinking of looking inside.

'Don't you have sisters at home, you monsters? Is this how you treat your women? You should be ashamed of yourselves! Bursting into people's homes in the early mornings! Making children cry!'

She was screaming now, and the soldiers – who had only recently left the protection of their mothers – were ashamed and a little scared. They turned and ran back up the stairs, shaking their heads at the captain.

'I apologize for the intrusion,' said the officer, and the search party departed as quickly as they had arrived.

Back in the well, Ali was suffering: his arms ached from holding on, and he was starting to go dizzy. He knew he should breathe more deeply, but the stale air seemed so unhealthy. He was delighted, therefore, when the lid was dragged to one side and he saw Rabab's face, smiling in the candle light.

'They've gone,' she said, extending her soft, henna-painted hands to help him out.

As he caught his breath, she ran upstairs, returning minutes later with a large, black *burka* and a padded bra.

'Take off your *deshdasha* and put this on,' she ordered, holding out the bra.

Ali understood the plan instantly, and although it conflicted with his manly pride, he knew it made sense. He undressed and pulled the bra into place, then waited while Rabab did up the clasp at the back and stuffed the large cups with socks. She pulled the tent-like *burka* over Ali's head, fixing the head-dress and face-veil in place. She then stood back and surveyed the results, nodding with approval and a smile of satisfaction.

'My Aunt Mona was a *very* big woman,' said Rabab. 'May God bless her!'

They went upstairs, and as Rabab put on her *niqab*, her elderly mother recited verses from the Quran. The children watched from the living room, dumbfounded.

The sun was just rising as Ali and Rabab left the house, walking through the cool, deserted streets arm in arm. Rabab hoped they might find a taxi and flee the neighbourhood before too many people were up and about.

'You must bend a little,' she told Ali. 'Try to look like you are old and in pain. Walk like an old woman. Shuffle a bit. That's right.'

They turned a corner and instantly wished they hadn't. Before them was a group of soldiers manning a check-point. There was no way out; turning around would look more suspicious than continuing. Rabab gripped Ali's arm tight.

'Just keep walking and follow my lead. Pretend to be ill. Grip your belly. I'll say we're on our way to the hospital. They'll let us through.'

Ali realized in a flash that he was unarmed. He had left his backpack behind in the cellar, and his pistol was inside. If things went wrong, he no longer had the option of shooting his way out. Either he played his part to perfection, or he'd be forced to run for his life.

The soldiers had seen the approaching pair and they had their weapons ready. As Rabab and Ali got within a few feet, a sergeant stepped onto the street from a nearby house, joining the team under his command.

'Where are you going?' he barked.

'My aunt is sick,' said Rabab. 'She's very ill. She had an operation but the stitches have broken. She needs to get to the hospital quickly, but we don't have a car.'

The sergeant looked deeply suspicious, stepping forward and squinting at Ali in the half-light. He peered through the fine layer of cloth covering the prince's eyes, and then at the large bosoms, which jutted out through the folds of black material.

He looked at Rabab and twisted his huge moustache. He liked to display his power in front of the young recruits, and even more so in front of women. From her voice and eyes, he guessed Rabab to be just a few years younger than himself. There was no harm in making a good impression.

'Bring the car,' ordered the sergeant. 'I'll take them to the hospital.'

They sped through the streets, bumping over the uneven tarmac, Rabab and Ali on the back seat, while the sergeant sat next to the driver.

They screeched to a halt outside the emergency department and Rabab helped Ali from the vehicle. The sergeant also offered his help, but his hands were mostly on Rabab, touching her waist and buttocks. Normally, she would have slapped him, but on this occasion, she was just happy that nobody was trying to grope Ali.

As they entered the lobby, a Filipino nurse approached, and the sergeant ordered her to provide the old woman with special attention. The nurse led Ali to a nearby seat, where he collapsed in apparent pain.

'Maybe I should take your telephone number, so that I can check on you later?' the sergeant asked Rabab.

'I don't have my telephone with me,' she said. 'Maybe I can take yours instead? Write it down for me.'

He took out his notepad and jotted down his number, handing it over. Rabab thought he had the look of a hungry wolf.

'So what's your name?' he asked, launching into his standard line of enquiry on meeting any attractive lady. He knew he could not date any woman from too respectable a family. Lower-class women were so much easier to conquer, particularly for a sergeant of humble origins.

She gave her answers slowly and guardedly, all the while drifting away from Ali, leading the sergeant back down the steps and onto the street. She wanted to put some distance between the two men. Beyond that, she didn't have much of a plan.

The nurse, meanwhile, had not been able to get a single word from Ali, only groans of pain. She looked for Rebab but she seemed to have disappeared. So the patient was loaded into a wheelchair and taken to a bay, the curtains closed around him.

'A doctor will be here soon,' said the nurse, and she walked off.

Ali's heart was pounding now. What was he going to do when the doctor arrived? Any physical examination would instantly reveal his gender. After which, they would no doubt discover his identity as their former ruler. At which point, all hell would break loose.

Clearly, there was no other option but to leave – and fast. He left the wheelchair and slipped through the curtains, turning right toward the exit. As he approached the lobby, he noticed the Filipino nurse talking with a doctor. Ali turned around and walked back the way he'd come, passed the bay, turning right at the end of the corridor. He had no idea where he was headed, but if he could find an exit, he might be able to walk along the street without being stopped. Perhaps he could find a taxi ... and just keep going.

Finally, there before him was an exit, the doors wide open. Ali walked through and started down the steps. He looked left and right, not sure which direction to take.

'Madam, wait!' said a voice from behind.

Ali turned and saw the nurse standing in the doorway. She was waving to him, clearly concerned that a sick, elderly patient would depart from the hospital without being properly examined. Next to the nurse stood a young soldier, smoking a cigarette. He said something to the nurse, who pointed at the escaping patient.

Ali decided it was time to get moving. He turned right along the pavement, back toward the front of the hospital. Maybe he would find Rabab there, and she could do the talking. He opened his stride, aiming to make the corner before the nurse and the soldier could catch up. He was aware that he no longer looked much like an old lady suffering from abdominal pains. He noticed also that his shoes – brown leather brogues from Jermyn Street – were visible, poking out from beneath his *burkha* every time he took a step.

He reached the corner and found Rabab more or less where he'd left her. The sergeant was climbing back into his vehicle, apparently pleased at having chatted up another woman. Rabab was standing on the hospital steps, waiting for the hungry wolf to leave.

Ali felt a firm hand on his shoulder. He turned just as the soldier ripped off his face veil. He punched the soldier full in the face, sending him flying back onto the pavement. The nurse looked up in horror, her face held in her hands.

Ali looked back at Rabab, who stood motionless, apparently frozen with fear. The sergeant opened the door of his vehicle and began to climb out. Ali looked at the nurse, who was muttering, 'Oh my God! Oh my God!'

The soldier was getting to his feet.

The sergeant reached for his pistol.

The nurse began to scream.

'Run!' shouted Rabab.

It was clearly now or never. Ali turned and started to run, gathering his skirts and sprinting down the street away from the hospital. He hadn't run for many years, and he was shocked to find that he was still able to do so. He noticed a strange rasping sound and then realized that it was his throat, gasping for air as his body strained to adjust. His chest began to burn, and he wondered if he might pass out before he was shot dead.

He was just approaching the next corner when he heard the first shot, and he was glad that there was no pain to follow. Apparently, the sergeant had missed.

Then he realized that this first shot was perhaps not meant for him. He turned and saw Rabab lying on the pavement a few metres behind him. She had been shot in the back. Ali ran back and tried to lift her as she gasped for breath.

The sergeant was going down on one knee, taking careful aim. Ali summoned all his strength and gathered Rabab into his arms, then turned and staggered onward. Another shot was fired and another. Ali thought the second bullet had hit Rabab in the foot, but he didn't have time to stop and check.

He turned the corner and saw a taxi parked by the pavement. The passenger was just paying the fare. With one hand, Ali opened the rear door. He threw Rabab onto the back seat and climbed inside.

'Drive!' he shouted. 'Drive! Drive!'

The driver looked over his shoulder, eyes wide. He looked down at the injured woman, whose blood was pouring onto the seat. He looked up again at Ali, wondering why the face seemed so familiar.

'There's been a terrorist attack!' shouted Ali. 'Drive!'

The cab driver understood now. He put the car in gear and sped away.

'Turn left!' shouted Ali, and the driver took the next left, turning down a side street.

'Where are we going?' said the driver.

'Shut up and keep driving!' shouted Ali. 'I'm with Military Intelligence. Just do as I say.'

The cab speed down the narrow street, bumping over potholes, the horn blaring as pedestrians scattered in all directions.

'Turn right!' said Ali, not sure where he was going.

The cab turned right and ran into another army check-point.

'Back up!'

'What?' said the driver.

'Reverse! Reverse!'

The driver had had enough. He opened his door and ran into a nearby café, taking cover behind the counter.

The soldiers at the check-point knew instantly that something was wrong. Nobody parked a car like that and ran for cover unless danger was near. Maybe it was a car-bomb; they were pretty much a daily occurrence now. The corporal on duty told his men to take cover, which they did, hiding behind concrete blocks, rifles clutched in sweaty hands – waiting for the explosion.

As they did so, the sergeant arrived from behind, his vehicle skidding to a halt on the dusty tarmac. He jumped out, waving his pistol high in the air.

'Don't shoot him!' he shouted. 'I'm taking him alive! We need him alive!'

Ali looked down at Rabab, who lay dying in his arms. He pulled back her face veil. She was really quite beautiful; he had guessed as much. Blood was foaming from her mouth as she gasped her last breaths. She looked into his eyes and tried to speak. Then she let out one long, final breath – and her eyes went blank.

She was gone.

Ali hid his face in his bloody hands and began to sob. Why did he bring misery to everyone who loved him?

Before long, he was sitting in the back of the sergeant's car, handcuffs on his wrists. The sergeant was looking very pleased with himself. He knew exactly who he had captured, and already he was anticipating the medal that he would receive. He had even started to compose his acceptance speech.

His reverie was cut short by the arrival of a colonel from General Intelligence, a man with a long, sour face and sunken cheeks. He wore a grey suit and smelled strongly of aftershave.

'I'll take it from here,' said the colonel. 'You're dismissed.'

'Thank you, sir,' said the sergeant, realizing now that if anyone got a medal, it would probably not be himself.

Chapter 22
A Deal with the Devil

'Is this really how you treat your prince?' demanded Ali. 'Is this how you show gratitude? Is this how you show respect?'

His questions were directed primarily at the General Intelligence colonel sitting in the front of the car, next to the driver. But he was also addressing the two beefy men either side of him on the back seat. They had been silent the whole journey, but they had not forgotten Ali's presence, leaning their bulky bodies against him and holding a blanket firmly in place over his head.

Ali had now recovered somewhat from the shock of his capture. Some of his former boldness was coming back, and it was expressed as outrage.

'Have you not read the Holy Quran? Have you no idea of loyalty, of a subject's duty to his earthly ruler? Don't you care about your religion, about your eternal souls? God sees everything. Are you not ashamed?'

The two men on the back seat listened impassively. They were no less religious than most people in the country, and they had indeed read the Holy Quran. But they thought it a bit rich of Prince Ali – playboy, adulterer, alcoholic – to be lecturing them on morality and religious duty. Added to which, as intelligence operatives, sympathizing with prisoners was not in their job description.

Ali began to struggle, but the men only linked their arms through his, holding him firmly in his seat. He could struggle all he wanted; resistance was futile.

Finally the car slowed down, passing through a rear entrance into the royal palace, the soldiers saluting as the colonel showed his identity pass. The soldiers were not particularly surprised by the passenger on the back seat, bent almost double, draped in a blanket. There had been quite a few of those over the years, mostly heading for the second-level basement area, equipped with jail cells and various technologies for making prisoners talk.

The car slid into an underground car park and came to a halt. Ali was blindfolded and yanked from the vehicle, then frog-marched down a flight of stairs and along a corridor. He heard keys rattling and a metal door opening. He was forced inside, the handcuffs removed. Finally, the blindfold came off, and he saw his guardians before him: two young men with close-cropped hair. Despite their determined handling of the prisoner, they now seemed a little embarrassed in his presence. Ali stared at them, but they avoided eye contact. There was a jailor too, an older man with a grey moustache and a bunch of keys. He looked likewise embarrassed. Ali thought he recognized the man from years gone by – but the name escaped him.

The three men were clearly keen to depart, and so they did. Before the door closed, however, Ali saw the colonel standing in the corridor, chatting quietly on his mobile phone.

'Yes, Your Highness,' said the colonel. 'He is safely in custody. Of course, Your Highness.'

And then the door banged shut, the key turning noisily in the lock.

Ali lay on the thin, dirty mattress and stared at the ceiling. He had no illusions about his future: he would not be released, and before death came, he might suffer horrible torments. He knew this place very well. His father had brought high-profile political opponents down here to be tortured, and the young Ali had been forced to watch. The idea was to prepare the boy for his future role: tyrant and tough guy, strongman and torturer, a man never to be challenged or defied.

However, the project had backfired. While Ali would never put up with disobedience, he had also been repulsed by what he'd seen in the dungeons, and his education in Europe filled his mind with new ideas: liberal values, religious tolerance, a certain easing of political constraints – perhaps even democracy of sorts. He felt certain now that it was this belief in a modern, democratic future that had cost him the throne. And his willingness to do business with China, of course.

Perhaps, after all, his father had been right? Only the wicked can hold onto power for any length of time. Those who show the slightest sign of weakness are doomed to be undermined. And it all ends on a dirty mattress in a dungeon, waiting for the torture to begin.

Ali slept for hours, awoke, paced his cell, passed water into a bucket, and then slept some more. There was a ventilation grill blowing in cool air, but no windows, and he had no idea of the time. Finally, he slept so long and so heavily that he began to wonder whether he'd been in the room for hours or days.

Then the jailer returned, opening a small aperture in the door and speaking softly. He had brought food and water. There was soap too, and toilet paper. These delights were passed through a larger aperture at the bottom of the door, the food arranged on a silver tray. Ali took the items gladly and began to eat. He was ravenous, and more thirsty than he'd realized.

As he ate, he examined the tray, which seemed suitable for a prince, decorated with fine engravings, either Persian or Indian. The food was also good, far better than he had expected: lamb cooked in a yoghurt-based sauce, all on a bed of rice. This traditional dish, known as mansaf, was among Ali's favourites, and he thought the choice was not entirely accidental. Someone still respected their prince, even if it was only a chef.

Ali's mind drifted back to the Arab Spring, to the particular day on which he had decided to flee the country. It was very hot, the tarmac melting on the streets, as crowds of protesters gathered to shout their slogans, calling for the fall of the regime. The police had been deployed in force, firing tear-gas into the crowds – but it seemed nothing short of a massacre would stop the protests.

Senior family members, chief among them Lolowa, had advised Ali to leave Jawhar, just long enough for tensions to be eased. Once tempers had cooled and certain reforms had been passed, he could return, they said. Lolowa was particularly insistent that this was the only way forward, and Ali had accepted the advice as well-intentioned.

Of course, once he was out of the country, a younger brother was shifted onto the throne, soon to be replaced by Yousef – and he had remained there ever since. Ali wondered how he could have been so foolish, so trusting. Had he learned nothing from his father and grandfather, who had worked so hard to teach him the ins and outs of politics and palace intrigue?

And now he was shut up in a prison cell, no doubt on the orders of Lolowa herself. Presumably, he thought, she would make an appearance at some point, if only to gloat.

'What a small world,' he murmured.

Satisfied by the meal, he fell asleep once more, but he awoke an hour later in a panic. What were they waiting for? If they were going to torture him to death, why not start immediately? And where was Lolowa? She was the power behind the throne, and if she had something to say, why not come and say it? Why delay?

He got to his feet and started pounding on the door.

'Where is Princess Lolowa? I want to speak with Lolowa now! Bring that bitch to me now! Can you hear me? Bring Lolowa to my cell! That's an order!'

Soon he heard the key in the lock and the door started to open slowly. He stepped back against the far wall, pressing his skinny body into the concrete. The jailer stepped inside, making way for the colonel. He was still wearing his impeccable grey suit, still looking drawn and deathly serious.

'What do you want?' he said.

Ali recognized the man now. This was Colonel Azam, a career intelligence officer, one of the sharpest political minds in the country. Indeed, many years before, Ali had helped Azam on his meteoric rise through the ranks. If memory served him well, Azam had been awarded a medal for his devotion to national security. It was Ali who handed over the medal, shaking hands with the serious-minded officer at a private ceremony.

And now the traitor was there before him, clearly having sided with Lolowa. He was a snake in the grass, an opportunist, a killer for hire.

'There's really no point in making such a fuss,' said the colonel. 'You are here for a reason and events will take their course. Banging on doors and shouting won't achieve anything. Surely you know this much from past experience?'

Ali took a deep breath. Of course, the colonel was right: he must remain calm.

'So what do you want from me?' he said.

Colonel Azam was on the point of replying when there was a commotion in the corridor. A door was being unlocked, and someone was shouting. It was a woman's voice, and Ali recognized it instantly.

Azam stepped into the corridor, bowing deeply as Lolowa swept into the room, flanked by two commandos in black uniforms and balaclavas. She looked as imposing as ever in her huge black *abaya*, the austerity of her clothing offset only by the Tiffany diamond rings on her stubby fingers. She pulled away her veil, revealing a puffy, contorted face. She stared at Ali, her painted lips forming into a grim smirk.

Ali broke the silence: 'So, are you happy now?'

'Wonderfully happy, thank you. I've missed you so much these past few years.'

'Well, finally you've got me back. You've accomplished your plan: seized power, humiliated my family, and thrown me into prison. You must be very pleased with yourself.'

'Yes, I'm very pleased, Ali. I'm very pleased indeed. You, on the other hand, don't look so good. You look rather tired, in fact. I'm sorry we couldn't provide more comfortable accommodation. Perhaps, if you had given us some warning of your arrival, we might have done better.'

'I'm bearing up, under the circumstances,' said Ali.

'Yes, but it's not what you're used to, of course. You'd much prefer to be living the high life, with your whisky and your sluts, insulting your religion, ruining Jawhar's reputation with every step.'

'How I live my life is none of your fucking business. At least I'm an honest man, and a good ruler. At least my people love me.'

Lolowa laughed. 'Well, that's debatable, I'm afraid. The feeling on the street seems to be that you're no better than all the rest: a drunkard and a tyrant – that's pretty much how you're remembered. You have a few supporters here and there, but they're mostly too shy to declare their intentions. Many of them are dead. But don't worry too much. There's really no point in worrying. Perhaps this will perk you up a little bit.'

Lolowa turned to the corridor and clapped her hands.

'Bring in the prostitute!' she shouted.

There was more commotion, and two more commandos entered, dragging Laura through the doorway and dropping her to the floor. She lay in a heap, sobbing.

Ali rushed forward, shouting: 'Laura! My darling!'

One of the commandos swung an uppercut into Ali's belly. The prince doubled over and crumpled to the floor, gasping for breath. The pain was shocking, radiating outward from his solar plexus, sending his body into one huge spasm. The commandos dragged him back against the wall, where he lay in the foetal position, wondering if he would ever breathe again.

'Leave him alone!' screamed Laura, looking up, her face wet with tears and sweat. 'Don't hurt him! Leave him alone!'

A commando stamped on Laura's neck with a huge boot, forcing her back to the floor.

'Handcuff him,' said Lolowa.

She was enjoying all this immensely, and she couldn't help laughing at the pathetic sight of Laura sobbing in a heap: such a strong, confident woman, reduced to a weeping rag-doll.

The commandos placed the cuffs on Ali and then stepped back, allowing Lolowa to come closer, looming over her captive.

She bent forward and spoke softly: 'We will do interesting things with your prostitute. And she will be just down the corridor, so you will hear every scream. How does that sound? Does it sound like fun, Prince Ali?'

'Leave her alone,' said Ali, still curled up tight but finally able to breathe. 'She has no part in this. She's done nothing wrong. Let her go.'

'Oh, but she's very much involved, my dear. You see, she came here to save you. And I thought it sounded like such a good idea that I even paid someone to facilitate her journey. The US government was very helpful too, as always. Everyone has been so very helpful. But it's primarily Laura's fault that she's here. She really should have stayed in New York.'

'You fucking bitch! Let her go!'

'Maybe I will let her go, Ali, but not just yet. First of all, we need a little cooperation from you. If you play very nicely, perhaps we'll put your slut back on a plane to America. If not... well, who knows what might happen. This country is so very dangerous these days. A pretty girl like that might easily be raped to death on the street.'

'Don't worry, they can't touch you. You're an American citizen,' said Ali.

'I came here to save you,' said Laura through her sobs.

Lolowa turned furiously and grabbed Laura by the hair, slapping her round the face.

'You stupid fucking bitch!' shouted the princess, switching to English for the benefit of her guest. 'Do you think this is some nice French movie? Is this some romantic movie where everything works out nicely in the end? A happy ending for you and your boyfriend? You're an idiot. You're really disgusting.'

She yanked on Laura's hair, slamming her head up against the wall, then motioned to the prison guards: 'Take her away! Do whatever you want with her. Have some fun with her. I really don't care.'

The guards grabbed Laura and dragged her down the corridor. She was screaming all the way, and Ali had to be held down by several commandos as he struggled to sit up.

'Now,' said Lolowa, 'let's talk business. I can do something for you, and you can do something for me. How does that sound?'

'Go to hell!' shouted Ali, still struggling furiously.

'Listen carefully, Romeo, because I'll make this offer only once. What I need you to do is make a statement in front of a video camera. We have the script all prepared. It concerns national unity – the need to unite against terrorism in these dark times. We will provide you with clean clothes. Just speak into the camera. Pledge your allegiance to my son and call on all citizens to do the same. If you do this, I'll put Laura on a plane in the morning. Refuse to make the video, and you'll both die very painful deaths. And I will be personally involved at every stage. That's the deal. Take it or leave it.'

Chapter 23
Enemy at the Gates

With the *jihadist* forces probing the suburbs, the city was on lock-down. The army had imposed an 18-hour curfew, allowing civilians just six hours each day to run errands, do shopping and fetch medicines. Some brave souls still struggled into work, but it was hardly worth the effort. Most businesses had closed and the roads were largely deserted. As the early-summer temperatures began to climb, the place had more in common with a Wild West ghost-town than a modern capital city.

Soldiers sat behind sandbags and atop armoured vehicles, nervously fingering their weapons and watching for unusual movement. Any civilians moving around during curfew hours were challenged. Those without written permission were arrested, and those who ran were shot. Such incidents were rare, however, with most people content to remain at home and watch TV. After all, if the city was to fall to *jihadist* insurgents, it would be on the TV news.

Reports from the front-line were not promising. Those army units responsible for holding suburban areas were on the back foot, being unused to full-fledged insurgent tactics. When the *jihadists* conducted a night raid, they typically claimed dozens of lives. During the day, too, they were effective, picking off army recruits with modern sniper rifles – supplied by their shadowy foreign backers. Shoulder-launch missiles had also arrived on the front lines, empowering the *jihadists* to take out army tanks, a terrifying development for the government forces.

The mood at the palace was only slightly better. The whole area had been fortified with concrete barriers and miles of razor-wire. Soldiers from the elite Royal Guard manned every gate and corner, crouching behind sandbags in anticipation of the battle that was surely coming. The minister of defence had stopped by to personally inspect the preparations, apologizing that no tanks had been available; all the heavy equipment was needed on the front line, he said.

The royal packing had long been complete, but Prince Yousef had so far refused to flee abroad. He was held in place by a certain sense of responsibility, combined with a dread of his mother's reaction to such a cowardly move. He sat in his private quarters most of the day, alternating between the television and his family, with occasional interruptions from anxious officials.

Lolowa, of course, insisted on fighting to the end – to the very last drop of blood. She had addressed the family and palace officials in the throne room, emphasizing the need for unswerving loyalty in times of national crisis. Indeed, she had reminded those present that any show of disloyalty would be interpreted as treason, the penalty for which was death.

In case anyone doubted her, there was evidence that same afternoon. Two members of the People's Council had been caught fleeing to the airport without permission from the interior ministry, a serious crime under the circumstances. Lolowa personally ordered their execution, and the deed was done by firing squad. Further arrests were made, targeting political figures suspected of sympathy with Prince Ali; their prospects of surviving in custody seemed slim.

However, if Lolowa thought she had asserted total control, she was mistaken. In a quiet corner of the palace's west wing, three middle-aged men sat around a marble-topped table. They were sipping coffee, as they normally did at this time of day. However, on this occasion, their voices were hushed, their manner secretive.

The eldest of them, Abdullah, was a cousin to both Lolowa's husband and Ali. Now in his late fifties, Abdullah had been heavily involved in ensuring the survival of Prince Yousef these past three years, helping to smooth the differences of opinion within the ruling elite. He was not only well connected, but known for his experience and worldly wisdom.

'She will alienate everybody,' he said, stirring more sugar into his coffee. 'That's if she doesn't kill them first. Those two executed for trying to flee were good men, important men with long careers behind them. They were simply thinking of their families. And anyway, the People's Council is suspended. What use was there in them hanging around?'

'You're quite right,' said the second, smaller man. 'Arrest them, yes, and possibly charge them with dereliction of duty. But executions on the spot? That's ridiculous. Lolowa has finally gone too far. She's gone mad.'

'But what can we do?' asked the third man, wiping coffee from his bushy moustache.

'Well, we cannot continue like this,' said Abdullah. 'If Lolowa is not curbed somehow, there will be nobody left to run things. She will eventually murder everyone with any experience. And there's no telling who she will suspect of treason next. It could be any of us.'

The three men glanced around, wondering for the moment whether they might be under surveillance.

'So what do you propose?' said the man with the moustache. 'We can hardly drive to the airport.'

Abdullah straightened his posture: 'Listen, I have a plan.'

The others listened intently, their mouths hanging open.

'My nephew, Mansour, is a major in the Royal Guards. He is in charge of the inner chambers of the palace, which includes the throne room, and the quarters of both Prince Yousef and Lolowa. Mansour is responsible for his own operations and the men under his command. And that includes the commandos who are guarding Lolowa night and day.'

'So, what will he do?' said the small man.

'All I can tell you,' said Abdullah, 'is that in the newspapers it will be reported as suicide. After all, the poor woman is clearly under a great deal of mental strain.'

His two companions smiled broadly. They were most impressed with the plan.

'May you live long!' they said.

* * *

Three days and nights had passed, and Laura had not yet been subjected to any form of torture. Every time someone came to the door, she expected it might start, but it never did. Instead, she found her situation gradually improving. At first, she had been forced to sleep on the concrete floor, but on the second night a mattress was moved in. On the third night, clean sheets were provided, along with a pillow and blanket, apparently freshly laundered.

Her meals were surprisingly good too, and she couldn't help thinking she was eating the same food as that served upstairs in the palace proper. She knew something was up when she was given lemonade instead of plain water.

Slowly, from a state of total despair, she managed to claw herself back to something approaching hopefulness. Before long, she was starting to consider her options, including possible means of escape. And in her experience, survival meant one thing above all else: manipulation.

At first, she attributed her improved conditions to the jailor: the tubby, middle-aged man with the grey moustache who had delivered the bedding and pushed her meal tray through the door three times a day. He seemed nice enough: quiet, gentle, and bit embarrassed.

Then, on the fourth day of her captivity, she found a new face standing in the doorway. It was an Army Intelligence officer with fluent English. He was good-looking, with honest eyes, and Laura guessed him to be in his yearly thirties.

He introduced himself as Captain Harith, saying that he had been educated at the Royal Military Academy Sandhurst, Britain's prestigious school for army officers. He was newly responsible for 'debriefing' operations at the palace, and he apologized for the grim circumstances of Laura's detention.

'We are not all monsters,' he said. 'Some of us have standards for treating prisoners – and woman generally.'

Laura was taken aback by the man's gallantry, and more hopeful than ever that manipulation of some sort might work. She would use all the seductive skills of

Delilah and win her freedom. But she would have to work quickly; she may only have one shot at this.

'I would offer you a seat, but...' she said, jokingly.

'Yes, I'm sorry, the furniture is rather basic,' he quipped back.

'Join me,' she said, sitting up one end of the mattress, her legs crossed.

Harith dismissed the guard and closed the door. Then, removing his shoes, he sat at the far end of the mattress, facing his beautiful prisoner.

'It's very kind of you,' he said, with a smile.

Laura knew men well enough to spot when they were attracted to her, and it was clear that Harith was already in the danger zone. She had only to lay on the charm a little more and he would become putty in her hands.

'I thought you were going to torture me,' she said.

'Please, madam, this is not going to happen. I would not allow it.'

'But I understand that this woman, Lolowa, is in charge. Surely, if she wants to torture me, she will simply issue an order?'

Harith looked uncomfortable, glancing around at the door behind him.

'I hope that it will not happen...' he started. 'I feel confident that it will not happen.'

There was an awkward silence, during which Laura played with the hem of her dress, gently stroking her smooth shins.

'Well, it's encouraging to be held captive by somebody handsome,' she said at last. 'That's something at least. I don't get to see many attractive men these days.'

'Not at all, madam.'

'No, really, I'm being serious. And you have excellent English, and some understanding of Western culture.'

'I have some exposure, of course. I love the English language. I have been to America too, several times.'

'Really? Where have you been?'

'To Washington and Miami. Also to Fort Bragg in North Carolina.'

'Ever been to New York?'

'Sadly, no.'

'Well, you must visit some time. I invite you.'

'Thank you so much,' he said, smiling broadly. 'That would be wonderful.'

There was another awkward silence, during which Larua played with her skirt again.

'You must be very afraid,' she said.

'Afraid, madam? Why would I be afraid?'

'Because of the fighting, of course. If the palace is taken over, you will be killed by the terrorists. Everyone will be killed.'

'We intend to fight to the end.'

'Yes, that's what I mean. Aren't you afraid of dying?'

'I am a soldier, madam.'

'But wouldn't you rather survive? I mean, what if you could escape? What if you could get to America? To New York, for example?'

Harith looked around again at the door, aware that the conversation was taking a strange turn that could be misinterpreted by anyone listening in.

'To New York? How?' he said.

'With me.'

'Madam, that is quite out of the question. My role here is...'

Laura leaned forward and gently lay a finger on his lips, pausing him in mid-sentence. She rose to her knees and shuffled forward, whispering in his ear.

'Harith, listen to me carefully. Regardless of your relationship with the royal household, when the fighting starts, you will be the last one they think to protect. They will save their own skins long before they save you. They will jump onto their private jets and fly away, leaving you and the other soldiers to die like dogs. Unless, of course, you have your own plan for escaping, a plan that includes me.'

She paused and looked into his eyes. He seemed simultaneously intrigued and alarmed.

'One good word from me,' she continued, 'and the US embassy will grant you asylum, along with your entire family. I will explain that you helped me to escape, and I'll tell them how kind and civilized you are. And when this palace goes up in flames, you will be in Central Park with me, eating ice creams. How does that sound?'

She sat back down again, legs crossed, and smoothed out her dress. She smiled her most conspiratorial smile. She had rolled the dice; she just hoped she'd rolled sixes.

Harith seemed to pull himself together, putting on a serious face and rising to his feet. He put on his shoes in silence and tied the laces.

'I'm sorry, madam,' he said, 'but I have other duties to attend to.'

'Just think about it,' said Laura.

The army officer left the room, locking the door firmly behind him.

* * *

That same night, Ali was squatting on his mattress, his wrists chained to the wall, wondering how he might escape from his terrible situation and build some sort of life afterwards. It was not only his incarceration that tormented him, but the fact that his reputation was ruined, his honour finally in tatters. More than ever, he felt gutted, empty.

Two days earlier, he had made the video statement, exactly as Lolowa had requested. He had shaved his stubble and put on clean clothes, then sat behind a desk in some nearby office. The wall behind him had been hung with expensive embroidery, a pot-plant positioned to one side. And he had read from the script, expressing his love for Jawhar, swearing loyalty to Prince Yousef, calling on the people to unite behind the young man in this moment of national crisis.

'If we all work together, we will defeat terrorism and rise from the ashes victorious, stronger than ever,' he had said.

He was quite sure there was no coming back from such a performance, which was perhaps even now being broadcast on TV news channels around the world. Those of his followers who were not fooled by the video would have guessed that he was in custody, most likely on the verge of execution. The game was over.

One silver lining, of course, was that he had not heard Laura screaming. Lolowa had said that if he made the video, Laura would be released. Perhaps this had already happened? Or perhaps she was already dead? While he had no hope of his own resurrection, he was desperate to learn of her fate – and to save her if at all possible.

He was snapped from his thoughts by footsteps in the corridor. The door opened, and there stood Harith, the polite army officer he had come to know in recent days.

'Master, I have brought your friend,' said Harith. 'She wishes to say goodbye.'

Laura dashed into the room, throwing herself at Ali and crushing him in her embrace, smothering him in kisses wetted with tears.

'My darling, my darling, my darling,' she whispered, 'I love you so much.'

'Laura, precious girl! I love you too... my precious girl.'

They hugged and kissed like never before, their bodies entwined, despite the obstacle presented by Ali's chains.

'But why are you here? What's happening?' said Ali at last.

'I'm being set free. Harith is helping me to escape. We're going to the embassy.'

Ali struggled to his feet and extended his hands to the young officer: 'You will be rewarded for your courage, Captain Harith.'

'I am at your service, sir.'

Laura threw her arms around Ali once more, planting more kisses on his face.

'We must go now, madam,' said the officer. 'We may be discovered. We should hurry.'

'But what about Prince Ali? We can't leave him here!'

Ali looked at Harith and held up his chains, which were bolted firmly to the wall.

'I don't have the keys,' said Harith. 'They are with Lolowa. I cannot set you free.'

'Break the chains!' shouted Laura. 'You must get him out. I'm not leaving without him.'

'But madam... the keys...'

'I will never leave without him. We live together or die together,' said Laura, a tone of panic now in her voice. She had really not anticipated that Ali would be chained to a wall.

Suddenly, Harith turned a looked down the corridor, eyes wide with fear.

'We must go now. Someone is coming. It may be Lolowa. We must hurry!'

'Go now,' said Ali. 'Save yourself. I will find another way to escape. But you must go now, before it's too late.'

Laura began desperately yanking at the chains, trying to dislodge the bolt.

'Take her away!' shouted Ali. 'That's an order!'

Harith darted into the room and grabbed Laura round the waist, yanking her into the corridor. She continued to struggle, fighting like a tigress, scratching at the officer's face. In the end, he punched her on the jaw, knocking her unconscious. He then threw her over his shoulder, slammed the door and walked away.

Ali slumped onto the mattress, his heart flooded with emotions: love, remorse, despair ... joy at the thought that Laura might actually survive this ordeal.

He heard boots marching along the corridor. The key rattled in the lock and the door flew open, Lolowa sweeping in, flanked by her bodyguards. Last of all, came the jailor, looking more timid than ever.

'Why did you pretend to unlock the door?' demanded Lolowa.

'Your Highness?'

'The door was clearly unlocked, and yet you pretended to unlock it. Why?'

'But the door was...'

Lolowa reached into the folds of her clothing and retrieved her diamond-studded pistol. She raised it to the jailor's head and pulled the trigger. Bone, blood and brains splattered over the wall and the man's body slumped to the floor.

Ali jumped to his feet, determined to strangle this evil woman, but he was wrestled to the floor by two commandos.

Lolowa stood over Ali, the pistol held casually in her bejewelled hand.

'Leave us!' she shouted, and the commandos left the room.

Ali lay in a heap, panting from the struggle, wondering now whether his time had come.

'So, the bird has flown from her cage,' said Lolowa. 'You must be very happy for her. But I can tell you now that you will never see her again. She will never make it to freedom, Ali, because even if she escapes me, she will not escape those monsters out there. Those terrorists will pull her apart on the streets. They will hang her naked from a lamp post and beat her with sticks.'

Ali managed an ironic laugh: 'You're so sad, really. You never miss an opportunity to hurt someone, to twist the knife. I should have put you down years ago. Laura is worth a thousand of you. She's worth a million of you. She's a good person. Even if she dies, she'll die a good person. You can't even begin to imagine what that means, you sick bitch!'

'Did I hear you correctly?' said Lolowa. 'Did you say that Laura is a good person? Oh, how wrong you are, you sad little man. Your little prostitute has been spying on your from the start, you idiot. Who do you think was passing information to the CIA? Who do you think was passing on your contact lists and recent phone calls? Who was printing out emails and handing them to the US embassy in Buenos Aires? How did I discover your entire network? Take a guess, you blind fool.'

'Do you really think I would believe that?' screamed Ali, beyond himself with fury.

'It doesn't matter what you do or don't believe. I'm only giving you the facts. Your sweet Laura is not only a prostitute, but a traitor.'

For a brief moment, Ali wondered whether it might be true. Perhaps she had betrayed him after all? Perhaps all those late nights and embassy parties in Buenos Aires had, after all, been part of a plot to undermine him? But why on earth would she do such a thing? Then he noticed Lolowa smiling down at him, a smile of pure wickedness.

'Go on and kill me then,' he shouted. 'If you're going to kill me, just do it. I'll be more than happy to join my mother at last.'

'As you wish,' said Lolowa. 'There's nothing else to say anyway. It's all over for you.'

Lolowa raised her pistol and pulled the trigger, sending a bullet into Ali's forehead and blowing a large hole in the back of his skull. As he slumped sideways into the mattress, she noticed that his eyes were wide open in surprise.

The princess stood for a while looking at the scene of carnage, drinking in the blood and gore. She breathed a deep sigh of satisfaction and swept from the room.

* * *

Five minutes later, she was in her bedroom, removing her chunky rings. She had already removed her *abaya* and was preparing for a shower. Somehow the day's events had left her feeling dirty. She had hoped her chamber maid would be here to help, but she seemed to be otherwise engaged. It was so difficult to find reliable servants these days.

As she closed the lid on her jewellery box, the bedroom door opened. Major Mansour stepped boldly into the room, flanked by four members of Lolowa's commando bodyguard.

'What are you doing in my bedroom?' she demanded.

Mansour couldn't help smiling to himself as he lifted the diamond-studded pistol from the bedside table and released the safety catch.

Chapter 24
No Heroes

Summer was in full swing now, with temperatures in the mid-forties. However, inside the luxurious five-star hotel suite, the air was cool, thanks to the efficient air-conditioning system that blew gently all day long. Laura had every physical comfort: a spacious bedroom; a sleek, modern bathroom; an elegant, well-furnished living room. Through the large windows could be seen a vast body of sparkling, blue water – much like the ocean in which Ali had swum as a boy.

But as she sat on the plush sofa, she was crying her eyes out. Four weeks had passed since her frantic escape from the palace, and she had travelled thousands of miles. And yet, she was still turning those horrific events over and over in her mind, as if by revisiting them should might change the tragic outcome.

She had spent the morning watching the TV news, seeking the latest updates on her beloved prince and his troubled country. She was tuned into her favourite Arabic-language channel, with its focus on the Middle East and the plight of the ordinary people, complete with English subtitles.

Today's update had hit her hard: confirmation of Ali's death, complete with a photograph of his face as he lay in a coffin. The bullet hole in his forehead was clearly visible, despite the application of make-up. Shaky footage had been shown too of the discovery of his body, allegedly in a 'private residence' on the edge of the capital. An official claimed the prince was murdered by terrorists, just days before the tide began to turn against them. Special-forces soldiers had apparently discovered the corpse as they pushed the terrorists out of the suburbs, bringing the capital and surrounding areas firmly under government control.

Officials hailed Ali for his self-sacrifice, saying that his video calling for national unity had helped to turn the tide against the *jihadist* forces. His somber message had 'brought the nation to its senses', providing the necessary impetus for decisive action. Prince Yousef even read a statement before the television cameras, honouring Ali for his selfless courage, calling him 'a true father of the nation'.

There was also an update on Lolowa's death. A health ministry spokesman revealed the results of the inquest, which found that she had indeed killed herself in a fit of depression. She had apparently been self-medicating in previous weeks, seeking to control her nerves as the fighting came closer to the city centre. The princess would be 'deeply missed by all who knew her', said the minister.

In light of these two most tragic deaths, Prince Yousef had declared that a week of national mourning would be observed – once the terrorist threat had finally been crushed in the provinces. He finished by thanking the international community, particularly the United States, for their firm support in Jawhar's hour of need.

Commentators sat in the TV studio discussing this latest US military intervention and what it meant for the region. A battalion of US Marines had been deployed, landing by air and sea, along with Navy Seals and a host of intelligence advisors. Attack helicopters buzzed over the suburbs, while F-16 jets ran sorties from the US Navy's aircraft carrier. Everyone agreed that this powerful military deployment has been the key to turning the tide against the terrorist forces that had brought this tiny country to the brink of destruction.

A former US general appeared, explaining that the US military was there on a short-term deployment aimed at 'establishing order' and boosting the government's existing military capabilities.

'Once this period of intense combat is over, we may see the US settling into more of an advise-and-assist role,' said the general. 'This event has demonstrated the important, long-standing ties between these two nations, particularly in view of the War on Terror.'

The channel cut to a press conference at the White House, at which a new 'intelligence sharing protocol' between the two nations was announced. At the end of her statement, the press secretary mentioned that a US delegation would be heading to the principality soon for discussions on oil and gas concessions. Back in the studio, one commentator observed that a recently negotiated gas deal with China would probably not be signed after all.

Every half hour, the news channel replayed the footage showing the discovery of Ali's body, and every time, Laura began to cry afresh.

'Farewell, my darling,' she said. 'I won't forget you.'

She lay on the sofa, burying her face in the cushions, curling up into the foetal position. She recalled her final moments with Ali and his insistence on her leaving without him. It was a final act of love on his part, confirmation of the depth of his feelings. But that hardly helped to quell Laura's anguish.

She recalled being dragged from the room and fighting with Harith, scratching at his face and then ... waking up in the back of a vehicle, wrapped in a blanket. She had sat up slowly, terrified and groggy, as the jeep sped through the city streets. Every now and then, they would stop at an army checkpoint, and Laura would hide beneath the blanket as Harith showed his military ID and drove on.

True to their agreement, Harith was heading to the US embassy. But as they approached the fortified building, he knew something was wrong. The street in front was swarming with soldiers and intelligence officials in suits and sunglasses.

'Get down,' he said. 'Get under the blanket. We can't stop here. It's too dangerous.'

They had driven into the suburbs and beyond, speeding through the front lines and into the desert. As evening came on, Laura wound down the window and breathed in the fresh air, feeling the wind of freedom in her hair. So much had happened, and all in a flash; now she was numb, unable to feel, unwilling to think.

The next morning she had awoken in a Bedouin tent, wrapped in blankets on a mattress on the floor. For a moment, she had no idea where she was. She had no idea of time or place – remembering only the basics of her identity. Then it all came rushing back: the horror, the heartbreak, the panic. And then the numbness that was the only sensible response to such trauma.

Soon an elderly woman appeared, bearing hot, sweet coffee, made with light-roasted beans in the local style. It was heaven to Laura, the first of several such gifts that would help to soothe her nerves in the coming days. The woman sat with her for some time, smiling and watching as Laura sipped her drink. Laura would look up occasionally, studying the tattoos on the woman's creased, weather-beaten face, struggling to guess how old she might be.

Laura was most surprised when the woman opened her mouth and started speaking in halting English, introducing herself as Harith's mother, Leyla. Within a matter of minutes, she had told the story of her parents and grandparents, all of whom had been nomadic shepherds. Her father was a respected, forward-thinking elder, and he wanted the best for his daughter, sending her to the village school, where she learned to read and write. Eventually, she married, but her husband was killed during the struggle for independence, as was her brother.

It was a terrible blow, but she had remarried, and God had given her a son late in life by way of compensation. Harith was the apple of her eye, a kind boy and very smart. He had likewise been keen to study, eventually earning a place at the military academy. It was his ticket out of the Bedouin lifestyle, but he had never abandoned his people, returning at every opportunity to see his mother and provide a little money.

Breakfast was brought in: warm bread, yogurt, beans and dates. There was more coffee and a glass of warm goat's milk. Laura ate hungrily as Harith's mother continued to talk, her soft, reassuring voice soothing away the anxieties. Laura was told of the Bedouin's ways, of their life in the desert, their work and pleasures, their rituals of marriage and their precious adornments. Laura lapped it all up, happy to hear anything that pushed out the dark thoughts.

Soon she was standing outside, blinking in the sun, surveying the rustic scene: a dozen low, black tents on a desert plain; goats roaming nearby, munching the sparse greenery; several beaten, old pick-up trucks; and women going about their business in traditional garb. Laura was dressed in a black *abaya* and headscarf, her face left open to the hot air.

She took a seat among a group of women, while Leyla picked up a garment and began to sew, peering closely as the needle darted back and forth.

'Where's Harith?' asked Laura.

'He has gone,' said Leyla, 'but he'll be back soon.'

It was a full week before Harith returned, this time clothed in jeans and t-shirt. He brought with him three modern 4x4 vehicles and several male relatives. They would be riding through the desert, crossing the border at a safe point, bringing Laura to freedom.

'We'll be leaving in two days,' he said. 'It's not absolutely safe, but it's your best chance.'

'What about Ali?' said Laura. 'Is he alive?'

Harith looked at his shoes, apparently struck dumb.

Laura knew the answer; she had known all along. There was no need for further discussion. Heartbroken, she returned to her tent and collapsed in a heap.

In the following days, the younger women helped her to prepare for the journey. The caravan would be seeking to avoid all checkpoints, but if they were unlucky, Laura must be able to pass for a local woman. She was fitted with a *niqab* that left only her eyes uncovered. Her face had caught the sun, turning a light bronze, and the women dyed her hair with henna, just in case a stray wisp should become visible.

Laura must be prepared to answer some basic questions that might be posed by policemen or soldiers. She was taught a few useful phrases in the local dialect, and the women giggled at her accent. Leyla said her Arabic was fine, the accent impeccable.

Finally, the evening of departure arrived, and Laura said her goodbyes to the women who had hosted her so kindly, hugging each in turn, saving the last and longest for Leyla. Then they started into the night, heading down increasingly bumpy desert tracks, until they were deep in the wilderness.

Just as the sun was rising, they emerged onto a flat tarmac road, and Laura was finally able to get some sleep. She was woken again as the vehicle parked outside a small house in a leafy suburb, where she was shown to a bedroom and told to rest. Within in a few hours, she found herself once more in the vehicle and then passing through the gates of the US embassy, declaring her identity and apologizing for the lack of a passport.

Harith said a hasty goodbye, offering a firm handshake and the best of luck.

'Perhaps we'll meet in New York?' he said.

'Yes, that would be nice,' she replied.

And he was gone.

The US officials were keen to debrief Laura on the events of the previous weeks, and she had happily complied, revealing all the details and holding back nothing. From time to time, they had switched interviewers, asking the same questions in various ways, searching for any inconsistencies or half-truths. In the end, they were content that her story was probably true, and they agreed to assist with her onward journey. She would be flown to Beirut, where the US embassy would continue to offer support and advice, but in more comfortable and secure surroundings.

Laura was pleased at this news. She had been to Lebanon several times, always enjoying the beaches, bars and cafes, as well as day trips into the hills. This time, of course, it would be different.

She was jolted from her thoughts by the telephone. She sat upright on the sofa and answered the call, nerves jangling.

'Yes, Laura speaking.'

'Hello Laura. This is Daniel Smith, the US ambassador to Beirut. I hope you're doing well.'

Laura was put on edge by the East-Coast accent and slippery voice. It was the sort of voice she associated with embassy parties, also with well-heeled men in hotel bars seeking to pick up high-class hookers.

'Yes, what do you want?' she said.

'First of all, I'm just checking that you're still safe and well. And second, I'd like to offer my sympathies for the death of Prince Ali. The news must be a terrible blow to you.'

The ambassador was saying all the right things, of course; Laura couldn't fault him on that front. He was, after all, a trained diplomat. But she sensed a deep insincerity in his voice, smooth words masking his true agenda. And she knew what the true agenda was: to ensure that she kept her mouth shut.

'Laura, are you there?'

'Yes, I'm still here.'

'I just wanted to say how sorry I am about...'

Laura cut him off: 'I'm going ahead with the press conference.'

'Are you sure that's wise, my dear?'

'Yes, I'm quite sure. It's happening in the next hour, and I intend to tell the whole story. I'm no less patriotic than any one of you. But people need to know the truth. I'm not doing this for myself, but for Ali. Also for the American people, who have a right to know what goes on.'

'And what about your country's reputation? I don't know what it is you think you're about to reveal, Laura, but if it's in any way harmful to the US government, it could be American citizens who suffer. Are you willing to jeopardize the safety of US citizens in the Middle East?'

'The world will be a better place if the truth is revealed,' she said, hanging up.

She walked to the large window and stood gazing at the Mediterranean. Before long, she was miles away, recalling scenes from her life with Ali: their first kiss in a bar in Geneva; relaxing in London, whether feeding ducks in the parks or reading the papers in Knightsbridge cafés; dancing the tango in Argentina; their furious arguments and gentle making up. Ali could be stubborn and pig-headed, but he could also be a gentleman and a sweet lover.

She thought of Harith, who had dragged her from the prison cell and punched her unconscious. She recalled his fear as they drove through the streets and his casual manner as they prepared for the desert journey the following week. What sort of man was he? He had saved her life; that much was clear. But why? What did he want? An attractive wife perhaps, or a new life in America? All men wanted something from a woman; nothing was given for free. This much she had learned.

There was a loud knock at the door.

'Come in!' she said, her voice simultaneously determined and tinged with sadness.

The door opened and in walked a tall, slim, lady with dark hair and a radiant smile. It was her old friend Cybil, arriving from the hotel lobby, where she had been briefing the assembled crowd of journalists, ushering them firmly into the conference room.

Cybil crossed the room with quick, confident steps, enfolding Laura in her arms.

'It's all ready: press releases, microphones, the lot. There's even a small buffet to keep everyone happy,' said Cybil.

Laura gripped her friend by the shoulders, saying: 'Thank you for your support, Cybil. I couldn't have done any of this without you. You're a complete angel.'

'All in a day's work, honey. Now, how about a drink?'

'Sure, there's white wine in the fridge. I'll get some.'

Laura poured two glasses of Chardonnay and the two sank into the sofa, Cybil closing her eyes in ecstasy as she took her first sip. She hadn't stopped for two days, and she wasn't used to the heat.

'So, are you sure you want to go ahead with this?' she said. 'There's still time to duck out, you know. Nobody would blame you if you did.'

'Yes, I'm quite sure.'

'You'll be accused of undermining national security, of course. That will be the State Department's line of attack, and they have plenty of friends in the press. Once you start on something like this, there's no turning back.'

'Yes, I'm ready for all that. It's not a problem. I didn't go through all of this only to have the truth covered up. Some people treated me very badly, and Ali too. And I'll be damned if I let them get away with it.'

'Fair enough.'

They sipped their wine some more, staring at the TV, which was once more showing the footage of Ali's body being discovered by soldiers. The sound was muted, but the subtitles were still flicking up in English.

'So sad,' said Cybil.

Laura turned to her friend.

'Cybil, do you remember when I first confessed my new profession to you?'

'Vaguely, yes.'

'Do you remember what you said?'

'No, what?'

'You said that if I believe I'm doing the right thing, I should go ahead – and never give up, so long as it feels right.'

'Did I say that?'

'Yes, you did. And on this occasion, I know I'm right. So that's why I'm doing it.'

'Well, there's your answer right there.'

Cybil drained her glass and stood up.

'Let's go downstairs and get this over with,' she said.

She held out her hand, and Laura took it. They left the room and headed for the stairs, keen to avoid the gaggle of hacks that would no doubt be waiting by the lobby elevators.

They crossed the lobby and entered the conference room, striding to the podium, where the microphones of various news outlets had been arranged. The two women stood side-by side as the cameras flashed and reporters rose from their seats, shouting questions.

'Please, ladies and gentlemen,' said Cybil, in her most commanding voice. 'Laura will read a short statement, and then we will have questions. But one at a time, please, in an orderly fashion.'

One prominent journalist could not contain himself and shouted his question: 'Laura, your actions are being described as heroic. How do you respond to that?'

Laura leant in to the microphone and spoke softly: 'There are no heroes in this situation.'

Printed in Great
Britain
by Amazon